The Dragon Prince

The Dragon Prince

VICKI BLUM

illustrated by
DAVID SOURWINE

Scholastic Canada Ltd.

Toronto New York London Auckland Sydney
Mexico City New Delhi Hong Kong Buenos Aires

Scholastic Canada Ltd.
175 Hillmount Road, Markham, Ontario, Canada L6C 1Z7

Scholastic Inc.
557 Broadway, New York, NY 10012, USA

Scholastic Australia Pty Limited
PO Box 579, Gosford, NSW 2250, Australia

Scholastic New Zealand Limited
Private Bag 94407, Greenmount, Auckland, New Zealand

Scholastic Ltd.
Villiers House, Clarendon Avenue, Leamington Spa,
Warwickshire CV32 5PR,

Library and Archives Canada Cataloguing in Publication

Blum, Vicki, 1955-
The dragon prince / Vicki Blum ;
illustrated by David Sourwine.

ISBN 0-439-95668-4

I. Sourwine, David II. Title.

PS8553.L86D73 2005   jC813'.54   C2005-901031-2

6 5 4 3 2 1   Printed in Canada   05 06 07 08

To Heather, Laura, Joanne and Sandy
— editors extraordinaire

"I am a brother to dragons . . . "
Job 30:29

CHAPTER 1

Ember of the Twenty-third Batch woke one morning to see a human standing at the foot of her bed.

At first she thought the tiny shadow was just the tail end of a dream, so she blinked a few times to clear away the fog. The figure remained stubbornly in place. At that point three things kept her from shrieking in terror and waking every dragon for six caves over.

One, the human was very small. In fact, if he had been any smaller he would have disappeared altogether behind the swell of her stomach that rose roundly beneath her snout. Of course,

Ember had heard all of the old horror stories that had been passed around for cycles — stories of young dragons cornered by humans brandishing swords or poison-tipped spears; dragon heads mounted on pointed posts; legs of dragon roasting over crackling fires. However, this human was too small to do much serious chopping and wasn't waving so much as a twig.

Two, the human boy was very dirty, blood-stained, and looked at any moment as though he might topple to the ground in a senseless heap. His clay-colored hair clung in globs to his tiny skull, his strange outer skin hung down in ragged strips, and his thin limbs trembled like a hatchling with a chill. All in all, it wasn't a sight to inspire fear, which brought her to reason number three.

The human child was weeping. A trickle of tiny tears carved its way through the dirt on his cheeks to drip upon the stones below. Several times he drew in a great shuddering gulp of air, then let it out with a sigh so deep and shaky she felt sure it was his last breath.

Still, Ember had serious reservations about getting involved. Pain-wracked and pathetic as the child was, to have even one small sample of Dragon Enemy Number One standing not three shortlengths from her bed was enough to set her scales a-quiver.

At one time her kind had ruled Callore and all of the lands beyond, but hundreds of cycles ago humans had stolen the dragons' magic. Once the skies of her world had been filled with dragons, but now only a few males could father offspring. Her race was slowly dying.

In spite of this, she had to admit she had never seen such a sorry sight as this small human being. In the time that it took her to raise her head, a stab of pity pierced through the hard crust she had built around her heart to the tenderness beneath.

This unexpected sentiment created a whole new problem. If she made any noticeable noise her brood mother would arrive in a clumping rush to defend her. For according to herd custom, until the present batch-cycle ended, she was still a youngling in need of protection. If the boy was found here, his chance of living out the day would be poor indeed, for it had been almost a hundred cycles since dragons and humans had had any kind of contact other than mutual pillage and slaughter. If discovered, the boy's life wasn't worth the head of a cornered cave rat.

Carefully and without making any sudden movements, Ember pushed herself up onto her haunches. The boy's eyes grew wide with fear but he remained staunchly in place.

"Who are you?" she whispered, as loudly as she dared. "Why are you here?"

The boy continued to stare at her with a look of barely controlled panic. "All right," she said, "so you don't understand me. I'm not surprised. You look like you're barely old enough to know your own language, let alone the Common Tongue. I admit the Common Tongue is difficult to learn. It took me half a cycle just to memorize the basic verbs."

She paused when she realized she was rambling.

"Well," she whispered, half to herself. "What now?"

Suddenly the boy spoke. Of course she didn't understand a word of it, but it came so unexpectedly and in such a sharp, high-pitched gabble that she jerked in sheer astonishment, cracking her head against the roof of the cave. She was flopped down in front of the boy, howling, when her mother lumbered in through the doorway of her cave.

Brood Mother scanned the chamber with keen eyes, ears and nose. Her level of skill would normally have caught the twitch of a mousekin's whiskers behind a pile of rock at a hundred short-lengths. Ember knew of nothing alive that could escape the prowl of an adult dragon. Brood Mother, however, was still half-asleep and somewhat distracted by Ember's bellows.

"Be quiet," she growled. "If you can still make noise, then you're fine."

She took one last glaring look around and addressed Ember again. "Next time be less blundering."

Brood Mother backed up, scowling as she went. Because Ember's cave was one of the smallest, and too narrow for her to negotiate a full turn, she had to shuffle awkwardly in reverse. This ungainly action was not in keeping with Brood Mother's usual air of propriety. By the time she reached the doorway a thin column of sooty vapor had begun to waft angrily from each nostril.

Ember was about to heave a grateful sigh of relief and sink back down on her bed of tuff-grass when her luck fizzled out.

The human child sneezed.

It happened too quickly for Ember to fake another sneeze herself, and Brood Mother was much too crafty to be fooled by such a manoeuvre, anyway. In a matter of seconds Ember had been shoved aside and the human boy was caught up and held dangling, hooked by Brood Mother's largest foreclaw, high over their heads. The boy screamed and struggled until he saw how far he had to fall. Then he merely screamed.

"A human!" howled Brood Mother, with such volume that Ember knew with a sinking heart there would be no dragon within a farlength left undisturbed. A dozen heads filled the cave opening. Brood Mother continued to wail and screech.

"I don't know where he came from," Ember tried to explain. "He just sort of turned up." But no one was paying any attention to her.

Then amid the clamor and confusion a ponderous silence fell. Ember shivered, knowing full well what was coming next. Only one dragon was capable of silencing the group with his mere presence and that was Ember's father, the sire and leader of the herd.

Ember sidled out of her cave behind Brood Mother and waited with bated breath as her father's great wings thundered overhead. She watched, trembling, as Herd Father landed on a narrow ledge as lightly as a great, bright swan touching down on water.

Even in the dim light of early morning he was magnificent and just a little frightening. Unlike the Scout dragons, who never grew as large and who would never have mates or herds of their own, Herd Father reached a full six nearlengths at the shoulder. His scale-skin was peafowl green, fading to a pale star-flower yellow on the underbelly. His legs and wings were twice the size of any Scout's, and it was rumored that even a humpback sea serpent would back down under the threat of those enormous jaws.

Herd Father's yellow eyes fixed on the sobbing child with a look that shook Ember right down to the tips of her clawnails. It told her that nothing she said or did would change his mind about the boy. The anticipation of the coming kill flared like fire in Father's merciless eyes.

"I found the human hiding in this youngling's cave," Brood Mother explained with an accusing stare in Ember's direction.

Herd Father's huge head swung around. "You," he rumbled, addressing Ember, "will remain in your cave for one full week without food or water, as punishment for protecting the human."

He turned back toward Brood Mother. "Take the boy to the feed pit," he ordered. "At sunset I will slay and eat him." Then without waiting for an answer (Herd Father rarely needed one, for his word was law) he spread his glistening wings, raised his great horned head, and soared off into the sunrise.

Nobody protested, for according to dragon law the judgment was fair. Among dragons, trespassing on another herd's nesting ground was considered an act of aggression. For a human to commit such an offence was no less than an act of war. The child wailed and reached out to Brood Mother with two tiny hands, but she dragged him away.

Ember slid back into her cave and huddled, shivering, against the cold stone wall. As the boy's cries quivered through the thin morning air, it came to her that dragon law would mean nothing to him. He would die without ever understanding what he had done to deserve it.

Ember remained imprisoned throughout the long, sluggish hours that followed. She paced back and forth in her small chamber, too restless to sleep. Flies buzzed around her eyes and snout; the air hung stale and thick. She watched as the sun labored listlessly up the sky, hardly seeming to move. Finally she could bear it no longer and crept from her cave.

By this time it was mid-afternoon, a hot and hazy part of the day when all the Scout dragons, save those posted on guard, were resting in preparation for the night hunt. Most did not doze in their caves during these summer months but preferred the refreshing coolness of the inner forest. She looked out at the trees running like a dark band through the valleys, and the hills swelling up like monstrous, mottled birth-eggs between them.

Inside that forest slept many of the unmated female dragons. Where Herd Father had gone she had no clue — no one ever said. Most of the hatchlings were clustered in knobby heaps by the water, where the strongest and fiercest of the brood mothers kept careful watch.

Ember slithered downward along the narrow ledge that overlooked the lake and the meadow to the feed pit beyond. She crouched as she moved, her stomach nearly touching the ground. A sharp stone raked over the scratches on her belly — the result of a recent encounter with a thorn-thicket. She smothered a cry between clamped jaws and carried on. Every ounce of her effort went into keeping completely silent, for any sound, however small, might be picked up by one of the Guard dragons and an alarm sounded. Violation of any of Herd Father's rules brought instant and severe punishment, especially a violation as blatant as the one she was presently committing.

Ember paused for a moment to consider why she was risking so much for so little, then once again recalled the shrill, hollow howl of the child fading off into the chilly morning like a question left unanswered, and she hesitated no longer. Of course she knew that his kind and hers would always be the most bitter of enemies. She disliked humans as much as the next dragon. But it was glaringly obvious, even to her, that this child was innocent of the crimes of his ancestors.

By the time she left the rocky terrain and entered the grasslands her legs had grown weak with the effort of crawling and were beginning to tremble. She rested only until she had regained enough strength to carry on. In time the going grew easier and the need for silence less acute, for the gentle swish of her body through the grass blended with the wind and the cries of the skylarks circling overhead.

That's when she should have remembered what Brood Mother had told her. Brood Mother often said that if anything could go wrong in a situation, it would. But Brood Mother's words were the last thing on Ember's mind as she neared her destination and sensed the feed pit only nearlengths away. Her speed increased. As she thrust her head windward to catch a hostile scent or, better yet, a glimpse of one or both of the guards, the grass in front of her parted with a sudden *whoosh* and she found herself gazing up into the snout of an angry dragon.

CHAPTER 2

It took Ember one heart-thudding moment to identify the dragon looming over her. It was only her childhood friend Brand. What she had taken for anger was merely his surprise at finding her where she had no business being, especially since she had been confined to her cave in disgrace.

Brand of an Unknown Batch was not a large dragon as far as dragons went. His egg had been found, only a few months before Ember's own birth, at the site of a nest massacre. At first the dragons who had discovered the slaughtered herd thought nothing could have survived. But as they continued to poke through the half-scorched tatters of flesh and bones and the scattered eggshells — a grisly, painful task — they came upon three unharmed birth-eggs. Only Brand's egg survived the return trip intact. It was never discovered who had destroyed the unknown herd, or for what purpose, but numerous theories sprang up in the days that followed. In the end the whole affair was blamed on humans, for lack of any evidence to the contrary.

Brand was almost a third of a batch-cycle older than Ember, but he and she had always been fairly equal in size and strength. Although Brand was small for his age, he was known for his expert flying and tracking skills. Yet, when it came to making the actual kill, he would often hold back. Brand never took the life of an animal unless it was needed for food, and he had always been unwilling to kill just because he could. This, however, was minor compared to what really set him apart from the rest of the herd and never allowed him to quite fit in.

Brand was the wrong color.

As far as Ember was aware, in the whole history of Callore there had never been a red dragon. Forest green ones, yes, and blues blending into purples, darkening to black. But if there was another dragon who looked like Brand, she had never heard of one. Of course, she and her herd-mates had become used to his strangeness as the cycles drifted by. None of them thought much about it anymore, which was just as well. Brand had always been a little on the shy side, and the one thing he didn't want was to draw attention to himself.

Brand stared down at Ember. She gaped dumbly back, wondering how to explain why she was dilly-dallying about the meadow instead staying in her cave as she was supposed to. As it turned out, she didn't get the chance. Brand had the truth figured out in an instant.

"The human is beyond saving," he said bluntly. "Get back to your cave before they hang you by your hindclaws from the tallest oak in Dark Forest."

Ember's next thought was to take flight, the only problem being that first she'd have to stand up — and Brand, being no idiot, would be on her before her horn-tips cleared the grass. It was plain as the snout on her face that she'd have to pretend to give in, and then wait until his back was turned to make her move. As she rose cautiously to all fours and faced him, eyeball to eyeball, she couldn't help but notice that she now topped him by a few shortlengths. If it came to an out-and-out battle, she had a fair chance of winning.

Brand stiffened and his eyes flared with anger and injured pride. He had guessed what she was thinking and clearly didn't like the idea of being bested by a female, even one who was his friend. Now was her chance, while he was unprepared. She plunged to one side. He caught her by the neck as quickly as a siecat snares its dinner and pinned her flat. Clearly he was not as unprepared as she had thought. With his teeth clamped gently on her neck and her face pressed snout-down in the sod, speaking was impossible for them both. After a few uncomfortable moments his grip eased and he raised his head.

"If you don't leave this alone," he warned, "you'll be driven from the herd, or worse yet, killed as a traitor. Is that what you want?"

"It isn't fair," she snapped. "The boy doesn't even understand what's happening. He's frightened and alone and he needs my help."

"Dragon law says he must die," Brand reminded her. "He's the enemy, remember? His people stole our magic. There's nothing you can do for him without risking your own safety."

Brand was right about the risk, of course. But somehow she needed to convince him that this human was different.

"I think he's an orphan — sort of like you are," she tried to explain. "Something must have happened to his family and he came here looking for help."

Brand let her go so suddenly that she tasted dirt. She coughed, then sneezed a spray of silt that rose like a cloud around her. She slid backward, trying to fend off his next assault, until she saw that no assault was coming. He had turned, but not before she saw the memory of his own painful loss swelling, like a ruptured wound, in his eyes.

"I can see that you won't quit until you're dead," he growled.

"That's right," she replied, realizing it for the first time herself. "I won't."

He stood for a long moment, his tail swishing angrily through the grass, considering her argument, puzzling over the right and wrong of it all. His breath hissed from his lungs.

"Tell me your plan," he said at last.

~ ~ ~ ~ ~ ~ ~ ~ ~ ~ ~ ~

Dusk had arrived. Ember had retraced her steps and lay pressed against the narrow ledge overlooking the large meadow and the feed pit beyond. At any moment now the human child would be turned loose to meet Herd Father. If this was done the usual way, and she saw no reason why it wouldn't be, a Scout dragon would drive the boy from the feed pit and out into the grass where Herd Father would swoop down and snatch him up.

Ember's plan to prevent this was a simple one. Brand would create a diversion. Then, while Herd Father was still distracted, Ember would dive from the ledge, scoop up the child in her foreclaws, and fly like a skua chased by the north wind. She had a vague idea that a mountain hideout might prove safest, at least for a time.

The human child was in sight now, teetering weakly atop a small clump of boulders, nudged onward by an impatient Scout. He slid down, picked himself up and stumbled through a sea of grass nearly as tall as he was.

Then Herd Father dropped from the sky like a great, glittering bird.

Brand's diversion came in the form of a wild boar that burst suddenly from a clump of bushes directly below. Brand was hot on its tail. The boar squealed in terror as it struggled to escape, saw Herd Father, shrieked even louder, and swerved in a new direction. Brand bellowed, spit fire, and swooped after.

Father, only a wingspan from the boy now,

didn't veer even a shortlength from his target.

Ember groaned inwardly and dived, not allowing herself to think, or she would realize that this dive could only end in her own death. Wind ripped at her face and wings and the earth spun. Then everything happened all at once.

A flash of red and the whistle of displaced air told her that Brand, always faster in flight, had abandoned the boar and was already several nearlengths ahead of her. Below, she saw that Herd Father make his final lunge, and she knew even Brand would never reach the ground in time. Then the boy screamed.

She was not surprised at the scream. Any creature faced with such a death would do the same. But what truly sent the scales rattling down her spine was this: the cry that came from the human child's throat was immediately followed by a sensation she had never felt before. It tingled like ice and fire in her veins, making her heart thump and her head spin. It only took her an instant to realize that this new feeling must be magic.

Herd Father, who was closest to the boy, took the brunt of the magic and was knocked senseless. His great body crashed like a pine in a gale. Brand, who was only a few nearlengths from the ground, flopped like a hooked fish onto the grass. A few

other herd members who were watching from a distance were thrown onto their sides. Ember, still fairly high in the sky, felt a zinging thrust through one side of her head and out the other. She spiraled closer to the ground, lacking the strength to pull free.

The magic disappeared as suddenly as it had come, and she was able to see the reason why. The human child had fainted.

Ember pulled out of the free fall, her heart thudding. She could hardly blame the boy for what he had just done. He had only been trying to save himself. But although it was a brave effort, it hadn't been enough. The moment he lost consciousness, his magic had disappeared. Herd Father was already struggling to rise and would shortly regain his strength. She had to do something, and quickly, but she was still too far away.

The next moment Brand lurched upward, clutched the child's limp body in his claws, and rose into the sky. With one last anxious look back, she soared after him to mount the southbound wind and ride it for all she was worth. Some time later, as the air cooled and the sun sank in a blaze of scarlet, she caught up with Brand.

"I'm here," she said, skirting alongside, "if you need me."

Brand dipped his snout in acknowledgement but made no reply. Higher and higher they climbed. Time droned endlessly on. The grasslands fell away and mountains swelled silver and purple against a cloud-streaked sky. The air burned thin and cold in Ember's weary lungs. The human child lay limply, cradled against Brand's chest, while the wind whistled around them.

"Hurry!" Brand urged.

"Where?" she called.

"To the mountains," he said. "I discovered something there on one of my long hunting trips. When I saw the boy, I knew that's where I had to take him, so I came up with a plan . . ."

"A plan?" she cried. "You came up with a plan?" Her chest heaved as she wrestled for air.

"Yes. I, too, intended to save the child," he explained. "I tried to talk you out of it because I didn't want you to end up as an outcast, without herd or friends. For me, it's not so bad. I already am."

She had no more strength to be outraged, only enough to follow him up and up toward what seemed like the very edge of earth and sky. They struggled on. Time passed. Then, when she thought the next sweep of her wings and gasp of her labored lungs would surely be the last, they arrived at the mouth of a cave atop the remotest peak in Callore. Thin air, hunger and exhaustion all played their part. She skidded across the ragged rock-edge and when the black fog of unconsciousness rolled in, she gratefully let it carry her away.

CHAPTER 3

Ember awoke to the flicker of fire on black, pitted walls and the spicy odor of human food bubbling in a pot. She gazed lazily around through half-closed lids at what could only be a dragon's lair — bare as wind-bleached bones but for a pile of tuff-grass in one corner and a clutter of odd but possibly useful objects in another. That dragons hoarded gold and gems plundered from wealthy humans was a story as old and many-layered as a heap of discarded skins. Most dragons saw the wrong in stealing, and those who didn't only took what could be eaten or put to some use.

Of course, there were exceptions to every rule and it was from these rare exceptions that the tales had sprung.

Ember lifted her lids a little higher and was immediately sorry. Her head began pounding with the intensity of waves breaking on rock, and her bleary eyes tried to focus on a scene that didn't make sense. It wasn't likely, in the world she knew, for dragons and humans to be found within the same set of cave walls. Quickly she closed her eyes and willed her churning stomach to settle.

The brief glimpse, which could not be trusted, had shown her Brand resting in one corner (to be expected), the human child sleeping (not surprising), an extremely old black dragon (doubtful), and three ugly humans with furry faces (impossible). She collected her thoughts and tried to imagine fields of grassy green, teeming with meadow mice too fat to run.

"You might as well open them," said Brand's mocking voice, breaking into her thoughts. "You saw right the first time."

She almost shrieked when the scene refocused. All three humans had moved nearer and were clustered about her head, peering down. They were even uglier up close.

She sucked in air and lurched to her feet. These

weren't children like the boy she had just saved, but dangerous, full-grown men. Instinctively the heat rose in her throat and her chest tightened for the blast. The humans scuttled like rats to the shadows.

"Wait!" came a rumbling protest. It swept the thoughts from Ember's muddled brain like the helpless tumbling of leaves before a storm. Her eyes met those of the great old dragon and were trapped in his fiery golden gaze.

"Those aren't your enemies, young one," he bellowed, "but humans who share my mountain home. They are my friends, and yours as well, if you'll only give them the chance. Take care not to offend."

"But . . ." She tried to comprehend what he was saying, yet even as her mind gathered the ideas, they scattered and were gone.

"Come closer!" he roared aloud. "My eyes are not as sharp as they used to be. Ah, yes. A fine young dragon, well fit for the task that lies ahead. Do you know me, Ember of Callore? Think, then tell me if you do!"

She stared for a long moment. "Cidrok," she whispered in awe.

It was true, then — not just a tale told to wide-eyed hatchlings clumped fearfully inside darkened caves. It was the story of a dragon hundreds of cycles old, a dragon filled with the earth's vast wisdom and strength. He had a mind so clever that he could, after only a few moments of knowing you, pluck your deepest inner secrets as easily as your own brood mother garners cone-nuts from a tree. They said he came only during the darkest, quietest part of the night and was so stealthy not even a Guard dragon would notice anything amiss. They said that if your thoughts were unkind or your heart full of deceit, in the morning you'd be gone, never to return.

Ember, of course, had always believed that the stories were merely fear tactics used by desperate fullgrowns to keep unruly hatchlings in tow. She herself had quit believing in the Cidrok story after half a dozen cycles, and had never taken a word of it seriously since.

Laughter rumbled from a mammoth chest and echoed hollowly beneath the vaulted roof.

"I hardly believe in me myself," he declared, raising an enormous claw to scratch absently at his gargantuan belly. "The tales have flourished over cycles of telling. No matter. The truth is even harder to believe."

Ember had lost the ability to speak. Her attempt at a polite reply rose to her throat in a tremulous mouse-like squeak. Cidrok carried on as if he didn't notice.

"You two younglings have created quite a stir, I must say. I've never known such a ruckus and there have been many in these long cycles, believe me. At the moment there's enough anger growing in these hills to bring the Great Sea to a boil."

His huge head waggled back and forth. "All of this over a human hardly large enough to stick between your teeth."

"But a very special human, my Lord," Brand said boldly, glancing at the sleeping child. "I sensed it the first time I saw him."

"I see," said Cidrok. "So now that you've brought him here, what do you want from me?"

"It seems we've come to you for help," Ember said, trying to make the most of her remaining shreds of dignity.

"Indeed. And how did you find me?"

"I followed Brand," Ember quickly replied, released at last from Cidrok's spell as he turned toward her friend.

"It was purely by accident," Brand told him. "I caught a glimpse of you on one of my hunting trips and figured out who you were. I respected your privacy, though. I didn't tell anyone about you, not even Ember."

The old dragon practically whooped. "You think you discovered me by accident? I doubt that, or I'd have every dragon in a hundred farlengths landing on my peak! But never mind. In time you'll understand better your own powers."

"Powers?" asked Brand, shaking his head in puzzlement. "What powers?"

"You haven't guessed yet?" rumbled Cidrok. "Surely you realize how different you are from other dragons. Haven't you always felt as though you never quite belonged?"

Brand just stared back at him, the truth naked in his eyes.

"I thought as much. Perhaps I can help you understand your own heritage better by telling you a story."

A story! There was nothing like a good tale to ease the tension and promote goodwill among dragons. Some of Ember's anxiety eased, though she was still careful to keep one eye on the men in the corner. When they were all more or less settled, Cidrok began his tale.

"Hundreds of cycles before either of you was born, dragons and humans lived together in peace. Although things weren't perfect and misunderstandings occurred, for the most part they got along tolerably well. In those days the entire land of Callore was united under one king, and that king was called a Dragon Lord."

"Dragon Lord?" Ember squawked from her spot in the corner. "Are you telling us that a human ruled over dragons?"

Cidrok ignored her protest and carried on. "Then something happened that no one foresaw," he continued, "least of all our innocent, trusting ancestors. A wicked Dragon Lord named Goran inherited the throne. He cared nothing for his people or for the dragons who served him. All he wanted was more riches and power, although he already had plenty of both. He would stop at nothing to get the things he craved — not even murder.

"A terrible war broke out between those who supported him and those who didn't. Unfortunately, a select group of dragons chose to side with him. No one knows the reason. Perhaps he convinced them that his cause was just. In the end, thousands of humans and dragons died and the once beautiful land lay in fiery ruins. From that time on, dragons no longer trusted humans nor would have anything to do with them.

"Once separated from humans, we gradually lost our magic. Thus the rumor was born that humans stole it from us."

"But they did!" Ember blurted indignantly.

Cidrok shook his head and continued: "The dragons abandoned their former masters and fled to the remotest parts of Callore. With no one to unite them, the remaining humans separated into tribes. Some chose to remain in FarNorth. The farmers and sheepherders settled in Grass Land, the woodcutters and artisans in Dark Forest. Here in the Blackrock Mountains, the humans survive by mining the rock and trading whatever they find of value with their neighbors.

"On the far side of the Blackrock Mountains is Desert Country. Many of the desert people are descendants of Goran and, to this day, feel that they've been terribly wronged. They have become a hard and vicious tribe, refusing to co-operate with their neighbors to the north and south. Between the desert and the Great Sea is a strip of semi-fertile land where more of these people have settled.

"And south of the Great Sea is Kowtow, a land of enormous cities and teeming industry. Kowtow is more heavily populated with humans than any place in Callore. Dragons never go there and haven't done so for hundreds of cycles."

"I've heard some of this before," said Brand. "except for the part about the Dragon Lords."

Cidrok nodded his ponderous head. "There's

more," he said. "Ten cycles ago a young prince of Callore, in order to prove his bravery and in obedience to the traditions of his people, set out to slay a dragon. At the same time, a young dragon, responding to an accusation of cowardice made by another member of his herd, decided to kill and eat a human. The prince and the young dragon chanced to meet one morning by the edge of Dark Forest. Both fought courageously and well, but in the end it was the prince who proved more cunning in battle.

"As the prince stood over the wounded dragon and gazed deeply into his foe's eyes, he saw not a dumb, vicious beast as he had supposed, but a gallant and clever opponent willing to die honorably and without fear.

"The prince paused for a long moment, then raised his sword to the sky for the death stroke. As the weapon fell, it was not the dragon's head that was severed by the blow, but a single hindclaw — to be taken as proof of the victory. After binding the wound with his own cloak, the prince departed for his own land.

"A few cycles passed and the prince became a king. One evening he was caught in an ambush and outnumbered by his enemies. Suddenly he was plucked from among them and lifted skyward by a dragon with a missing hindclaw.

"From that time onward an unusual friendship developed. The dragon and King Briais, as he was named, became fast friends. Although they both spoke the Common Tongue, they learned to know and love each other so well that eventually they could speak without words. Then there came a day when the king and the dragon decided the feud had gone on long enough, and the time had come for all dragons and humans to reunite and work out their differences. From that day they worked hard to bring this about."

Ember snorted. "Even if your story is true, the peace you speak of could never happen. Your own words prove that humans can't be trusted."

Cidrok's head snapped back and something like anger flared deep in his amber eyes. "Curb your tongue, young one," he rebuked her. "You speak of things you know nothing about. Times have changed. The past must be put behind us. King Briais promises that someday soon dragons will rule alongside humans."

Ember doubted that, but fearing she'd already said too much, she kept her unwelcome opinion to herself.

Glancing around, she saw that the child had wakened and was staring around, his eyes wide and bright with confusion. Then his gaze settled on Cidrok, who must have too closely resembled the Herd Father of his most recent mishap, and he let loose a series of high-pitched howls. Three small men immediately stepped out from some dark corner of the cave and rushed toward him, bearing gifts of gooey human food in bowls, warm, soapy water, and a change of false outer skin. Ember stared in fascination. She had known for a long time about the false skin but had never seen it actually removed from a human's body until now. It was no wonder they wore it, she noted with pity as they peeled off the child's outer layer. The real skin underneath was as thin and fragile as the inner sac of a birth-egg.

Brand spoke. "Your tale is very interesting," he said politely to their host. "But what does it have to do with us, or with the child?"

"The child, as you call him, is named Shadrel," Cidrok informed them. "As for the relevance of my story, think about it for a moment. I've dropped enough clues to make the truth quite clear."

Ember was about to remark that she had never been very good at puzzles of any sort — dropped clues or not — then thought better of it.

The conversation halted again as the humans paused before them, holding plates heaped with assorted meats and vegetables. As a general rule, dragons ate meat, but on occasion Ember had enjoyed a romp through the potato-bulb patch or a good chew on the inner bark of a cacao-wood tree. The vegetables offered looked edible enough, she had to admit, and smelled even better. She eyed the men nervously, but it wasn't until after they withdrew that she began to eat.

"I've got it," Brand announced some time later.

"Indeed," said Cidrok.

"Shadrel must be the son of this King Briais you speak of," Brand declared. "Perhaps the king was killed, or driven into hiding by his enemies, and the son, by amazing luck, has escaped. And you, Cidrok, are the dragon who befriended this king!"

"Not bad," said Cidrok. He picked at his teeth thoughtfully with one long foreclaw.

"But that doesn't explain everything," puzzled Ember. "How did Prince Shadrel find us? Where is his mother? Is his father still alive? How was he able to use magic at such a young age? Where did he — ?"

"Enough!" rumbled Cidrok. "One question at a time!"

"Am I right?" Brand persisted.

"Yes — and no," Cidrok said. "You're right in that Prince Shadrel is the son of King Briais.

Because of his love of dragons and his desire for peace, the king made many enemies among the desert people — who believe to this day that they were betrayed by the dragons. They raided his castle, murdered his queen, and threw him in his own dungeon. The king's trusted aide, following a plan worked out earlier, fled with the prince toward a place of safety. They never arrived. The king's aide died of wounds he received during the rescue and the prince, alone and lost, stumbled upon your herd."

"And the king?" wondered Brand.

"Stone walls and iron bars could never hold such a king. Having been told that his son was murdered along with his aide, he escaped and departed with his loyal followers — to where, no one knows. But you are wrong on one important account."

Cidrok held up one hind foot, then the other, to show that he had no missing claw.

"The dragon who befriended King Briais disappeared as well," Cidrok told them sadly. "It seems he has gone into hiding, but where is a mystery."

Ember had just realized one of Cidrok's most annoying habits. The more questions the old dragon answered, the more new puzzles he managed to create. How did he know all of this stuff, anyway?

She could ask, of course, but somehow she doubted that he'd tell.

Cidrok and Brand continued to chat as Ember
watched the fur-faced humans leave the cave and
return moments later with some bags. Two of
them carried what looked like large pieces of animal skin with strips and loops that dangled down
on either side. She had hardly begun to wonder
what use they could possibly have when she heard
Cidrok explaining to Brand that his human friends
had made the objects and that they were called saddles.

"The saddles will be tied to your backs so you

can safely carry Shadrel and one of my men," he said calmly, as though this sort of thing happened every day. Ember let out a howl of protest and headed for the cave opening. Cidrok was one wingflap ahead of her. The next moment she found herself pinned flat against a wall, unable to move, with the end of Cidrok's great tail wrapped around her neck and his teeth a shortlength from her snout.

"Listen to me," he growled. At this range, his teeth were enormous indeed. "The long-awaited time has arrived. This journey is more important than you realize, and your part in it is vital to the future happiness of all creatures. You will carry the supplies that are required. Brand will take Shadrel, as well as Yemah, my human friend of many cycles. You can trust him. He will guide you well. You will travel south through the mountain passes, over the desert, and across the Great Sea to Kowtow. I believe this is where the king has gone. It's the only place where the boy will be safe. You have a kind heart, Ember of Callore, and great courage. Use it to overcome your prejudice of humans, as I know you can. You've already made a good beginning by saving the life of this boy. Do you believe me?"

Ember would have nodded if she could have moved. When he let her go she slithered to the ground and lay there, shaking and wheezing for breath. Brand threw her a look of sympathetic understanding, but remained silent.

Several humans began to stuff food and extra false skins into bags, which they tied to one of the saddles. Ember stiffened as they hoisted the supply saddle onto her back between her wings and secured a strap around her chest.

Just as they had finished tying the empty saddle on Brand, another man stepped inside the cave. To Ember, all humans were strange and ugly, of course, but next to this one the others looked almost attractive.

A patch of his head fur had fallen out, leaving a round, bare area on top. His snout was large for a human, and beneath it his mouth was hidden in the mass of fur that covered half his face. He was so skinny it seemed to her that someone had stuck some knobby sticks together to make a man. But when he looked at her, she saw a strength in his eyes that reassured her.

The next few minutes passed in noisy confusion as Yemah and two other men tried to convince the nervous little prince to climb onto Brand's back, but at last the boy was in place with the calm-faced Yemah behind him. Brand emerged from the cave with his new burden, and turned to nod farewell to Cidrok. Ember followed him out onto the rock-edge, stretching her wings and preparing to launch. She could see that Brand's eyes were bright with the anticipation of adventure, and she felt ready to join him in whatever lay ahead.

They departed as the sky paled to a hazy rose and tiny snowbirds fluttered from their nests to greet the day.

CHAPTER 4

Ember had plenty of time to think about her past and present failures as they flew.

"You're so impulsive," Brood Mother had often told her. "I'm afraid that some day it will get you into serious trouble." Well, that day had come, and the worst part was, Brood Mother was no longer here to rescue her from her own foolishness. She wanted Brood Mother to know that she had finally learned her lesson and she planned on telling her so. If she lived through this, that is.

On she flew, Brand and his passengers just ahead. Above, a flock of brown and silver skylarks dipped and soared while sunlight sparkled off their wing tips and the limpid luster of the morning sky haloed them in blue. She watched, fascinated by their grace and beauty, and her problems, though not forgotten, were for the moment pushed to the back of her mind.

In the early afternoon they slowed down, descending to a canyon in a range of rocky peaks below. Ember had never flown so long without stopping for a rest, although she knew it was common enough for the Scout dragons during their overnight hunts. The muscles of her shoulders, chest and wings throbbed, and she was happy to lie on a wide expanse of rock, sucking in the thin, cool air. After this small respite, she wondered if she would be able to lift off or simply plunge weakly to the ground below.

Yemah slid off Brand's back and reached up to lift Shadrel down. Ember watched as the man limped stiffly over to her side and rummaged in the bags for water. The boy bounced at his side, relieved to be free of the confining saddle. It seemed she wasn't the only one with cause to complain.

Airborne once again with his human cargo in place, Brand teased Ember by gloating about the superior strength of male dragons. She lunged for his tail but her teeth snapped shut on empty air. Groaning, she considered chasing after him, then gave it up. It would require too much effort.

By nightfall Ember knew there were no words in the Common Tongue, or any other language, to describe how weary she had become. Slowly they descended to a wooded crest of land and settled in a clearing. Yemah pulled the bags from her back and dug out some food for Shadrel. She dozed off once while Brand hunted for their meal nearby. He brought back some freshly killed rodents of an unknown kind, roasted them with his fiery breath, and placed them beneath her snout. She dozed off twice more while lying face-first in a pool of drinking water. Some fuzzy, faraway corner of her brain told her that the mountains had melted into gentle hills and her body lay upon the springy softness of soil and grass rather than on cold, unyielding stone.

That night she dreamed. It was the same dream she always had, but this time it was more frightening than ever. She lunged from her ground-bed in terror, flapping and clawing at the air, and saw Yemah crouched on the slope of the hill, keeping watch. His pale eyes were fixed upon her, burning with a steady glare. A great howl gathered in her throat, but Brand sensed it and lunged. The blow

knocked the breath out of her like a plunge in a cold lake, and with it died her cry. The last few wisps of the fright-dream faded and were gone. She stood before her startled companions, shaken and gasping.

"Quiet!" Yemah hissed, his strange, human eyes glittering like ice beneath the light of Callore's triple moons. "If any of your herd have followed us, they'll hear you. Our enemies are everywhere — human and dragon!"

"I'm sorry," she mumbled, turning away. She sank back, still trembling, onto the grass.

"Ember," came Brand's quiet voice beside her.

She kept her face turned away from him and pretended not to hear. The last thing she wanted right now was his opinion — or his pity.

"Tell me about your dream," he said. "Talking helps me sort things out. Maybe it will do the same for you."

She remained as she was, not moving or speaking.

"Have it your way," she heard him mutter. She knew Brand was only trying to help, and that made her feel worse than ever. But she just couldn't bring herself to talk about it right now. The minutes and hours crept by, and it wasn't until the sky had paled to an ashen gray and the stars had been devoured by the dawn that exhaustion overcame her and she slept.

~ ~ ~ ~ ~ ~ ~ ~ ~ ~ ~ ~ ~

They breakfasted on a variety of small rodents that Brand had toasted to perfection with a few breath flames. Prince Shadrel crouched nearby, clutching a sliver of dried fruit in his fist, and stared. As the slurping and crunching continued, he let out a laugh, and before Yemah could stop him, he had grabbed a chunk of Brand's meal and sunk his tiny teeth into it.

Yemah's eyes widened in alarm and he yanked

the food away. Then he dragged the boy to a safe distance and whispered something in the human language. Shadrel listened gravely, his eyes fixed on Ember and Brand. After the lecture was over the boy kept his distance, but Ember couldn't help but notice that a few smiles and giggles continued to appear, and the bright eyes followed Brand adoringly.

She had to admit that Shadrel could be charming, but she feared all the charm in Callore would never bridge the rift between humans and dragons. In spite of what Cidrok and his friend, the king, had said, her kind were just too different from theirs. And then there was the sticky problem of the stolen magic. She shivered and tried not to think about Shadrel's stunning scream — a scream that had toppled half a herd of dragons and sent the rest fleeing in terror.

Later, when Shadrel and Yemah had finished their own meal, Yemah packed everything up and strapped it on Ember's back. Shadrel squawked in protest as Yemah helped him onto Brand, clearly unhappy to have his playtime come to an end. Once settled, he seemed to cheer up at the prospect of flying again. Ember's lift-off was a little strained, but as she flew the soreness gradually worked out of her back and wings. Brand was at least considerate enough to set an easy pace.

By noontime the green landscape had faded to dull brown. Then a huge desert swelled and dipped below them like a vast golden sea, throwing back the sun's potent heat in a sharp shimmer of light. Finally Ember was forced to turn her head away, her eyes half-blind and burning.

They landed in the shade of a few scraggly trees upon the only bit of grassy landscape they could see for several hundred farlengths. Ember resisted the impulse to roll over and tear the clinging saddle from her back like an old scab. She couldn't help but wonder why someone as clever as Cidrok couldn't come up with a better system, one that didn't pinch or chafe her tender belly skin. However, she did have to admit the humans needed something to sit on besides rough scale and backbone. And they needed something to hang on to. Without the saddle they'd be left behind on the first swoop.

Ember drank deeply from a shallow waterhole, then moved aside to make way for Brand. The humans had slipped off his back and Yemah bent to scoop a cupful for the boy, then one for himself. Next, he made sure the waterskins he carried were filled. Though dragons could eat and drink enough to last for several days, Ember was learning that humans, apparently, could not.

She searched for a patch of shade large enough to stretch out under, but saw that Yemah had already claimed the biggest for himself and the prince. Very well, she would be content with shading her head and neck only. Perhaps if she curled up small enough she just might squeeze in her wings and forearms. After twisting and squirming, she relaxed into a half-comfortable position and closed her eyes.

"Ember," said Brand, as he settled down beside her. "How are you feeling?"

"Better," she said, as she peeked at him through half-closed lids.

"I want to talk about your dream," he said bluntly. Tact was a trait that Brand had never managed to master.

"Forget it," she snapped, turning her head. "It has nothing to do with you."

"I disagree. When your dreams become so strong that they put your life in danger, then it has very much to do with me. I care about your safety."

Ember stiffened, her teeth clenched. He didn't say his own safety as well, though she was smart enough to know that it was affected, too.

"I think it would help to talk about this," Brand continued calmly. "Don't be embarrassed — I've already seen bits and pieces of your dream. I didn't intend to, but it just sort of happened. I can't explain how."

Ember sighed, dug in her claws, and choked out the words. It was clear he'd never let her rest until she did.

"In the dream I'm always lost with my sister," she said. "We're still hatchlings, too young to fly. We've wandered from our brood mother and are hopelessly lost. For a while we run in circles but then we become too tired to go any farther. Suddenly a group of humans — perhaps seven or eight of them — surround us so we can't escape. At this point in the dream I sometimes wake up with fright, but not often. The next thing I know the humans take sticks and stab us in our bellies. We howl and howl. That's when I usually wake up."

There. It was out. Maybe now he would go away and leave her alone.

"What happens when you don't wake up?" Brand persisted.

She should have known he wouldn't let her off the hook so easily. "One time the dream ended differently," she admitted. "The humans kept poking us with their sticks, but they weren't trying to hurt us. I know it sounds strange, but it was almost like they were playing with us — trying to tickle us.

Then all of a sudden Brood Mother came hurtling out of the sky, spitting fury and fire. The humans ran in terror. Fire blazed all around us. We ran, too. That's when we got caught in the thorn thicket."

"That's about what I thought," Brand said. "Since last night I've been thinking about you and watching. You've been taught all of your life to despise humans. We all have. But your dreams have made those feelings even stronger. I think you're reliving an event that happened many cycles ago. And your mind is fighting against itself — the brave and kind-hearted Ember who rescued the helpless boy against the angry, frightened Ember who believes humans are, and will always be, her most bitter enemies.

"Do you know what I think? We're almost full-grown dragons now. We're old enough to follow our own instincts. We're in a situation where we have to travel with humans. Let's watch them. Talk to them. Get to know them. Then you make a judgment of your own, based on what you see and feel, not on what someone else has told you. Maybe then your nightmares will go away."

Ember lay there for a time, and when she finally raised her head to tell him that maybe he was right and she would think it over, he had gone to nap in his own small patch of shade.

CHAPTER 5

They left the oasis behind just as evening fell over the land like a blanket of gray silk. Since then they had covered more farlengths than Ember cared to think about. Her muscles ached with fatigue as they glided over the gloomy landscape searching for a place to rest. Prince Shadrel had chattered and sung to Yemah in his squeaky little voice for most of the night, only falling silent closer to morning. She was amazed that he had slept at all, with the wind in his face and the steady throb of wingbeats in his ears. To make matters worse, the night was chilly and the moons — delicate and beautiful — were shrouded in clouds, offering little light to see by. Just before she saw him fall asleep she heard him whimper, and her heart went out to him.

Brand circled above the dunes, searching for danger, then settled groundward. Ember looked in vain for a rock, a tree or even a cactus to cast some shade, but all she saw was the gentle sweep of the sand stretching in all directions, pale and never-ending in the morning light. With a sigh she landed next to Brand on a piece of ground as bald and bare as a newly laid birth-egg.

"Nice spot," she declared, gazing around. "The only problem is, we stand out like tic-flies on a zebu's rump."

"It makes me nervous, too," Brand admitted. "But what choice do we have? We can't go much longer without a rest."

He was right, of course. A half-hour later Yemah had everything unloaded and was preparing to make some breakfast for himself and Shadrel. Ember wondered if she would ever get used to the strange way humans overcooked their food. It seemed to her that when they were done, all that remained was either a dry, chewy husk or a gooey mess. She looked away, gazing out over the sand. Not a stick of firewood in sight, she noted. A flicker of flame escaped from one nostril. Perhaps she should offer to cook his meal for him. It would give the poor humans a chance to taste food the way it was meant to be.

She should have remembered what Cidrok had said about Yemah. The wise old dragon had known this man for many cycles and would never choose a guide who wasn't resourceful and well-prepared. She might as well count on the fact that Yemah would continue to anticipate every problem. Out from one of his large bags came a small, man-made object which, when rubbed with his thumb, produced a small column of smokeless blue flame. Ember stared in surprise, trying not to be disappointed that Yemah wouldn't need her help after all.

A few minutes later, Brand returned from searching for food with several large sand snakes dangling lifelessly from his jaws. Ember normally preferred rodents to reptiles; however, out here in the middle of the desert one couldn't afford to be too fussy. When roasted with her breath, the snakes were tastier than she had expected, or perhaps she was just hungrier than she realized.

Drinking was a luxury neither she nor Brand were able to indulge in — not unless they found some water, which seemed unlikely. This wasn't a serious problem at the moment. Dragons, unlike humans, were quite capable of going up to a week without water, and Ember and Brand could wait.

The sun, by this time, had grown from mildly warm to definitely uncomfortable, and it was still early in the day. Even Yemah with his bag of tricks couldn't hold back the might of a world's sun, Ember feared. Dragons were less sensitive to extreme heat than most other creatures, for their scales were designed to reflect sunlight. But they were not invulnerable, for once a dragon's scales were heated beyond a certain point the dragon could literally cook to death inside its own skin. It wasn't something she liked to think about.

Yemah was digging around inside his bag again. Ember lay listlessly in the sand, wondering idly how she would ever make it through this long, miserable day. The man had found what he was looking for. Out from the depths of the sack he pulled a strange-looking skin, the likes of which she had never seen before. It crackled like dry leaves when he unfolded it and glittered silver in the sunlight like the surface of a lake. When spread fully out, it looked large enough to cover twenty men his size. Yemah saw her staring in puzzlement and explained in Common Tongue, "It's a special material designed by our most skilled inventors to reflect the heat." Then he nodded in satisfaction and paused, as if he expected her to give his people the praise they so rightly deserved. Ember resisted the urge to move back from the strange, magical object. She tried to reassure herself that its purpose was to help and not to hurt.

Next Yemah took out several silver sticks that, when pulled upon, grew longer and longer. When he was pleased with the length he attached the huge skin by its corners to each of the sticks, stuck them into the sand, then trudged around the entire affair prodding and pushing until he seemed satisfied.

"Go underneath," he commanded. "It will help — trust me."

Shadrel ran under cover and, reluctantly, Ember followed. Sure enough, she immediately felt cooler in the skin's shade. She began to believe that survival and perhaps even sleep might be possible. She stretched out, sighed wearily, and let her mind drift. The last thing she remembered was Brand being ordered to stand guard and Yemah informing her that she would have to take the second watch.

~ ~ ~ ~ ~ ~ ~ ~ ~ ~ ~

Brand woke her early in the afternoon.

She slithered out from under the skin. It was as

if a bolt of lightning had struck her right between the eyes. She squinted, allowing a sliver of light to filter between her lids. Her vision adjusted. She saw nothing but the same monotonous lack of anything that breathed or moved or grew. Slowly she moved off to scout to the east. Some time later, checking south, she noticed the dust. At first she thought some distant breeze might have caused it, so she stood at full height and raised her snout to the scalding air. It was as heavy and still as the lull before a thunderstorm. Something other than wind had stirred up the sand, and it was clear to her that she'd have to take to the air for a closer look.

Up she rose into the brightness. The resisting air burned rather than cooled as she skimmed over the rippled sand. She maneuvered up a rise of land and labored to retain her height. The ground plunged steeply below. Another hill loomed. Up and over she went, struggling like a hatchling on its first flight. Her lungs heaved; her wing membranes stretched taut with effort. At last she found what she sought and almost toppled groundward in alarm and dismay. Moments later she was back, tearing frantically at the magic silver skin.

"Wake up!" she cried. "Humans are coming! Wake up!"

Brand and Yemah leaped from their sleep.

Yemah grabbed the saddles, threw them on her back and Brand's, and fumbled frantically to cinch them. Shadrel huddled near Brand, puzzled and fearful, as Yemah ran to take down the skin shield. The seconds dragged, but at last supplies, boy and man were in place and ready to go.

They lifted to the white-hot sky. Already Ember could see the tiny figures of the humans below, their heads and bodies protected by their false outer skins, hurtling across the desert on the backs of their windmounts, while the sand sprayed up in a dusty belch around them.

The windmounts, Ember noted with unease, were of a size and variety she had never seen before. Windmounts were not an animal that was found naturally in Callore, although their cousins, the wild horses, thrived in abundance upon the plains and lower foothills of the country. It was thought that the desert people had bred the first windmount hundreds of cycles before Ember was born. They had flourished like prickleweed ever since. It was a well-known fact that they were the only creatures (other than men) capable of defeating a dragon in battle. When cornered they fought like worgs, slashing viciously with their great, ringed horns or striking out with sharp, deadly hoofs. Their skulls were thick, their eyes dark and dull, and their hides so tough it took several blasts of fire before they even noticed the heat. Not only that, they could run like nothing else on four legs. Only speckleback cheetahs were faster, but the cats lacked the endurance of windmounts and in any contest were soon left far behind.

Ember followed Brand's lead as he rose almost straight upward in a struggle for height. The riders and supplies were now a handicap, for without them she and Brand could have risen more quickly. Ember spared a quick peek down. She knew these men weren't from Callore, for the people of her homeland were farmers and sheepherders, more likely to be bumping along in a wagon pulled by a plow horse than astride a fleet-footed windmount. No, these were the desert men of Cidrok's tale — those enemies of King Briais that the old dragon had warned them of.

It took all of Ember's strength to keep up with Brand. Her wings pumped as her breath hissed from her lungs. She saw with dismay that the human swarm had started to make some headway in closing the gap on her. It was unheard of for windmounts, fast and tireless as they were, to gain ground on dragons in full flight. Unheard of, that is, until now, for gaining they were — not by much, but enough that her chest tightened in fear.

The only way of escape was to rise high enough that the humans could no longer reach them, but that wasn't happening quickly enough for Ember's comfort.

Brand, as usual, had a plan all of his own, for he suddenly banked, then swerved off in another direction. Ember almost shrieked in alarm, then saved her breath for flying higher. The fool was trying to confuse the men, giving them all the chance to get away. It would never work. He would just get himself killed. A second later her hopes soared. Brand was a skilled flier — he might just pull this off and save himself as well. Now Ember saw that the group of men had come to a full halt below them. Arms were raised, weapons pointed skyward. She almost whooped aloud, sure they had lost their chance. They had waited just a few seconds too long. The deadly arrows from their bows would not reach to this height, and if a few managed to make it they'd carry about as much punch as a Zylian honey bee.

Brant had circled back, and they were now passing over the main cluster of humans. Arrows filled the air below and zinged around her head and shoulders. One or two thumped against her chest, repulsed by the hardness of her scales. She felt a tiny sting on her underbelly where the scales thinned to skin. She scratched at it and the arrow came free in her claw. It was small and pathetically thin, hardly larger than a blade of tuff-grass. She flung it away and adjusted her balance, feeling almost sorry for the creatures below, for their pathetic underestimation of a dragon's strength and endurance.

Ember struggled on, becoming aware of the stifling heat, the spinning sky, and the ground that seemed to be rising toward her like a swollen wave. Through a rapidly thickening haze she realized that her wings no longer pushed air, her lungs no longer sucked it in, and her body was engaged in a crazy one-sided tilt. She felt herself drop from the sky like a rock.

Everyone was screaming all at once — the men below with wild ecstasy, Yemah with horror and dismay as he and Shadrel clung to the saddle, and Brand in helpless rage as he swooped frantically toward her. She tried to right her body and to align her wings but neither would respond to her command. She knew, with a kind of dull dismay, that the men had used their terrible magic to bring her out of the sky. A few more moments and it would all be over. The least she could hope for now was to land upright, taking the brunt of the shock with her belly down, hoping there was

enough strength in her legs to cushion the fall.

She made one last enormous effort to spread her wings and felt them reluctantly respond. The wind caught at the membranes and the terrible dropping slowed but did not stop. Time and luck had run out. With dismay she realized that she was still too young and inexperienced to correct her downward plunge this close to the ground. The last thing she saw as she struck and slipped into oblivion was a sea of cheering human faces.

Chapter 6

Ember woke with a dreadful pounding in her head and an ache in every bone. A brief look around showed her that she was stretched out on her side on the sand, with her wings tightly wrapped and all four claws securely bound. Brand and Yemah lay close by, equally trussed. They were all beneath one of those large skins on poles that the humans liked so much. All, that is, except little Shadrel. Beside her, Yemah was speaking in angry growls to Brand.

"There was poison on the darts," he muttered sourly. "I should have warned you they would do something like this.

I have failed in my duty to the prince and to my people."

"It's too late to worry about that now," said Brand practically. "What we need is a plan of escape."

Ember's head hadn't quite cleared yet, but what Yemah seemed to be saying was that the humans had brought them down with poisoned arrows. Where were they? And where was Shadrel? The anger rose inside of her. Her chest swelled with heat. One good blast would certainly burn away the ropes, but unfortunately dragons were not immune to their own fire and she might do them all more harm than good. She knew she couldn't break them, for she had already tested their strength. Under different conditions she might have been able to free herself, but her tumble from the sky had left her weak and bruised — in body as well as in spirit. A glance at the marks on Brand's stomach showed her that he, too, had come within range of the arrows.

"We would never get away with it during the daytime," Yemah was saying. "They would just shoot us down again."

"We'll wait until dark, then," advised Brand. "But unless we can free ourselves, we're defeated before we begin."

"Can you reach the ropes with your teeth?"

A pause. Then, "No. Can you?"

"Even if I could," Yemah declared, "it's likely the ropes would outlast my teeth. A man's teeth aren't built for such vicious work."

"I have an idea," said Brand. "My teeth are stronger than yours. Move closer. I might be able to chew through the ropes around your hands."

The conversation got no further, for the next moment a man approached over the dunes, pulling Prince Shadrel along behind him. The man was large for a human, and the parts of his body not covered by false outer skin were dark and lined from years of desert living. The moment he released Shadrel, the boy darted across the distance to Yemah.

Their captor's huge body shook with rage. Words barked out through broken teeth. Yemah replied in the same harsh tongue. The man growled and barked again while Shadrel trembled and wound his arms tightly about Yemah's neck. It seemed as if the human's grumbling and grunting would go on forever, but at last he shook his fist, spit into the sand, and departed with a final scowl and an ill-aimed kick at the boy, which landed instead on Yemah. The sickening thud of boot on bone set Ember's teeth on edge. For someone to be

so callous, especially toward those of his own kind, was enough to turn her stomach.

"What was that all about?" Ember quizzed Yemah in disgust. "What does he want us for? Why doesn't he speak the Common Tongue?"

Yemah shook his head. "The desert people have always chosen not to speak the Common Tongue. They believe their own language is superior."

"I see," said Ember, not really seeing at all. She feared that the ways of humans would never make sense to her.

"They've set up camp nearby. That's where they took Shadrel. He isn't co-operating," Yemah continued to explain. "The prince is terrified, of course. He won't eat or drink. He won't speak. They need information from him. It's probably all that's kept him — and us — alive. After they get what they want, they'll have no more use for us."

"Do they want you to convince him to talk?" asked Brand.

"Good guess. I have until sundown."

A heavy gloom settled upon them. The silence lengthened. The hours dragged, until finally Ember slept out of sheer boredom. She woke some time later to see Shadrel curled up between Brand's legs, with his head against the dragon's belly. Brand would be surprised when he woke up. It was such a touching sight that her eyes stung and a lump thickened in her throat. She choked down the unwanted feelings and glanced at the sky. The sundown Yemah had mentioned was nearly upon them. Fear thudded inside of her.

"What else did the human say?" she asked Yemah, as Brand began to stir. Maybe they had overlooked something important — some tiny clue that could get them out of this alive.

He cleared his throat with a growl. "The human scum had one or two irrelevant opinions."

"Such as?"

"He took the time to comment upon my appearance and the appearance of all mountain men in general."

"Oh?"

"He said what I most look like is the back end of a Sifian donkey."

Ember had thought she was beyond laughter, but she felt it bubble up to her throat in spite of herself. Beside her, Brand hooted and thumped his tail in the sand. Shadrel, who had wakened and was watching them all with wide, serious eyes, felt the mood lighten and burst into a tinkle of bubbly laughter that fell through the air like cool rain. It wasn't until Ember heard Yemah chuckle along with them that she realized how close she was coming to liking him. She still felt a little reluctant to trust him completely, but he had shown that he could laugh at himself, an ability that even some of her own kind lacked.

But now Yemah was serious again. "These men are after the king's sword and the king's crown, which are symbols of power and of great worth. With them, no one can dispute their right to rule Callore. They didn't find them in King Briais's abandoned castle and they believe the prince knows where they are hidden. He doesn't, but he does know that these men are not nice and he's frightened. He wants me to make the men leave him alone. He wants you big dragons to break the ropes and carry us away from this bad place. But most of all, Prince Shadrel misses his parents."

"I could use a few of those myself," Ember agreed, imagining masses of maniac brood mothers scattering men before them like cave rats before a pack of hungry wolves. Then another picture filled her mind — one of Herd Father flat on his back in the meadow, knocked senseless by magic.

"Yemah," she said, her heart rising. "I can't believe I didn't think of this sooner. Ask Prince Shadrel to use his magic to free us!"

Yemah stared at her blankly for a moment, then shook his head.

"You don't understand," he said. "It doesn't work that way. The boy doesn't have any magic of his own."

Ember shook her head in frustration. She was about to tell Yemah that she had seen Shadrel use magic with her own eyes, but she never got the chance. A company of armed and angry men surged across the sand toward them. Ember couldn't understand the shouted words, though her imagination filled in all that she needed.

"Your time is up!" the leader must have said, as

he pressed the tip of his sword against Yemah's scrawny neck. "Tell now, or die!"

Yemah gulped as the sharp metal pricked his tender flesh and croaked, "You can't force us to tell you something we don't know!"

The point pressed deeper; blood beaded on his skin, then trickled down in a crimson trail.

The crowd of men swarmed around, shoving and shouting. Swords were drawn. Metal clanged. Prince Shadrel's thin, high wail rose above the din.

Ember turned her head, trying to catch a sound that hung just outside her reach. Yes, there was something — a deep background noise — a low rumbling that seemed to come from above them and all around them. It swelled, and in seconds all other noises were snuffed mute by what could only be the beat of a million tiny wings. The humans' windmounts screamed and strained against their hobbles. Their terror could only mean one thing, and Ember found herself following the premise to its clear and logical conclusion.

The only danger that could throw a herd of windmounts into such a mindless panic was the arrival of desert locusts. True, a swarm of the smaller variety would only nip and gnaw their way past without causing more than a few red itchy blotches on the underbelly. The giant locusts, on the other hand, were another matter entirely.

Then she saw the swarm and knew, with heart-failing certainty, that these predators were of the larger kind and that nothing in all of Callore could save them now. Those humans who were farthest from the direction of the approaching cloud had a chance of escaping astride a good windmount. On foot, a man's chances were poor at best. The only thing she and her bound companions could hope for was that it would all be over as quickly as possible. Once the locusts arrived, it would only take minutes for their bones to be picked clean and smooth as a newly-laid egg. It was rumored that death by locust consumption was relatively painless after the first few bites, due to the natural anesthetic found in the saliva of the insects. It was an interesting theory but since no one had ever lived to confirm it, it remained only a theory.

The men fled toward their windmounts, all interest in kings and crowns swept away by the sheer terror that overwhelmed them. Locusts swarmed across the skin shield in a black wave. Their rate increased. The sand around Ember writhed. She felt the snap of the tiny jaws as they clicked harmlessly against her scales. It was only a matter of time, she knew, before they attacked the defenceless skin of her belly. She and her companions had ended up trading one enemy for another, and it had been a poor trade indeed.

Prince Shadrel had fallen and lay face-first in the sand. As Ember watched through horrified eyes, Shadrel pushed himself slowly to his knees. Locusts covered his body like a dark, writhing skin. Yemah howled and rolled toward the boy. The man, too, had almost been enveloped by the crawling mass. Brand thrashed helplessly, trying to break his bonds. A few moments and it would all be over. What did she have to lose? Better burned than dead. Ember focused her will and felt the fire grow within her.

"Wait!" Brand cried.

Prince Shadrel was standing fully upright now. A shimmer of magic filled the air. Locusts dropped off his body like cone-nuts from a tree. Yemah and Brand, as well, had suddenly been released. The locusts slid from Ember's own torso and scooted away. The insects now swarmed across the sand and through the air in every direction but no longer touched the four of them.

"Don't move!" hissed Ember frantically. "Don't even blink or they might come back!"

"It's all right," said Yemah, quietly. "They won't come back. It's the magic that's making them go."

"You said he had no magic," Ember growled

from between clenched teeth. "Why did you lie to me?"

"I didn't lie," Yemah snapped.

"Where is it coming from, then?"

"I'm not free to say."

Ember clamped her jaw tight to keep from howling in frustration. Beside her Shadrel grinned with glee as he chattered and pointed happily at the scattering locusts.

"What's he saying?" she asked.

"He's telling the bad bugs to go away," Yemah explained.

Excitement and relief washed over Ember. She wouldn't have believed this if she hadn't seen it with her own two eyes. Here in front of her was all the proof she needed. Yemah obviously had no idea what he was talking about. She strained at her ropes and huffed: "Well, the least Shadrel could have done was order the locusts to remove these insufferable ropes."

Brand pushed himself up onto shaky haunches and his eyes met Shadrel's. In an instant a few hundred of the insects turned in the air and landed on the knots. Moments later the ropes sprang loose like stretchwood, falling in tangled heaps about their feet.

Somehow, Ember realized later, Shadrel must have understood — and decided to act.

CHAPTER 7

It took some rummaging to find their badly mangled saddles and supplies amid the scattered wreckage. What the men hadn't ransacked the locusts had chewed to ruin. Yemah mumbled sourly as he sorted the tattered remains, gathering bits of things from various places until he seemed almost satisfied.

The night grew dark around them as they rose into a sky spattered with stars and moons. Below them the dark blotch of the insect mass moved across the desert like a swiftly spreading stain. Men and windmounts fled before it in an ever-widening arc. Most would escape; locusts swarmed only at dusk and dawn, then disappeared into the sand that spawned them, like wisps of vapor that melt beneath a noonday sun.

As the hours passed, Ember could no longer find it within herself to complain about the difficulty of the journey. Difficult was good. Sore and weary was marvellous beyond words. Sore and weary meant she still lived, breathed and flew.

They arrived at the desert's edge just as the sun slid cheerfully forth to greet them. With their backs to a bluff, they bedded down upon tuff-grass under a leafy cone tree. In no time at all Prince Shadrel was curled up fast asleep, breathing deeply. Yemah stretched out wearily beside him as Brand began the first watch. Ember was bone-weary almost to the point of stupor, yet found sleep somehow eluding her. After a lengthy session of flip-flopping on the lumpy ground, she gave up and went in search of Brand.

"It's about time," he said when he saw her. "You've been fuming and fretting again — I can see it in your eyes. It's not healthy to keep all those feelings locked up inside. If you're not careful, you'll end up with a bad case of stomach burn — "

"I didn't come to get lectured," she said. "I came to ask your opinion, if you don't mind."

"You're afraid," he said, as if arriving at this dazzling conclusion had been the result of great insight. "We're all afraid. Who wouldn't be? We've fought against our own Herd Father, we've been shot out of the sky by an army of men on windmounts, and we've nearly had our bones picked clean by locusts. You've held up very well, considering."

"Brand," she said, interrupting his well-meant pep talk. "Yemah lied to me about Shadrel having magic, and he won't admit it."

Brand had found a tree with some sharp knobs on its trunk and began to scratch vigorously against it. Grunts of pleasure emerged from his throat. Ember had to bite her tongue to keep from howling in frustration.

"Are we talking, or not?"

"Can't I talk and scratch at the same time?"

Ember turned and stomped back towards the camp. The scratching ceased. "All right, all right," he called. "I'm listening."

Ember didn't feel much like talking anymore but she gave it another try.

"Yemah lied to me," she repeated.

"Maybe," he said. "But Yemah might believe he's telling you the truth. He sees things differently than we do. He's the first human we've spent any time with, and we've always known they're not like us. You need to focus on the things that matter. The locusts are gone. We're alive and healthy. I'm sure this misunderstanding you've had with Yemah will sort itself out in the end."

"I guess you're right," Ember muttered, half to herself. "But I keep thinking about Shadrel and his magic. We've been taught to hate humans because they stole our magic, but Yemah denies that it ever happened."

Brand had found another tree and was scratching again. Ember sighed, knowing she was beaten. The discussion had been very unsatisfying. She turned, and without a parting word staggered back the way she had just come. She was dimly aware that Brand had abandoned the tree to follow her, but she was beyond caring. She arrived back at camp and sank into the grass. The last thing she remembered was Brand peering curiously down at her while the jackdaws circled above his head, glinting darkly in the early morning light.

~ ~ ~ ~ ~ ~ ~ ~ ~ ~ ~

She woke in late afternoon to the sound of Shadrel's laughter and the smell of dragon-roasted meat. Brand's hunting skills had definitely improved since they had left the herd, even if nothing else good ever came of this mission. She had noticed, however, that he only went after the smaller game like rats and hares, and left the larger, more intelligent animals untouched. "They're too much like us," he had said when she mentioned it. "They don't just live by instinct. They're self-aware. Can't you feel it?"

Ember, who hunted very little because that was primarily a Scout dragon's job, didn't know what to think. She remained wisely silent.

Her strength returned as she ate, and when the food was gone, they got ready to leave. By nightfall they stood upon the shores of the Great Sea.

Ember had been listening to stories about the sea since the day she first struggled from her egg. It was said that the Great Sea was deep, so deep that it would crush your bones to powder if you were lucky enough to survive its brutal cold. It was said that no creature had ever escaped when caught in a storm upon the Great Sea, for the wind screamed in agony, lifting the waves to such heights they dwarfed even the tallest human ships and could dash one to splinters in a breath. It was said that even the humpback sea serpents cowered beneath the waves at times like those. Ember, however, was doubtful that a sea serpent would ever cower beneath anything. Any creature that was ten times the size of a dragon, could spew out a lethal torrent of sea water, and swallow full-grown whales in a single gulp was not, in her opinion, about to be frightened off by a few waves and some wind. The sea serpents were, in fact, rumored to be distant relatives of dragons. On occasion she had heard them referred to as "dragons of the deep." It was a rather bold supposition on the part of the dragons, she figured, and one that she had never taken too seriously.

Yemah had dismounted and was making sure everything was in order for the crossing. After a bit of digging around in one bag he produced a small metal object which he held out before his face and then squinted down at, all the while slowly turning it this way and that. The prince chattered eagerly beside him.

"Is it just my imagination, or does Shadrel feel more at ease around us now?" Ember asked, as she and Brand reclined on a patch of level ground to snatch some rest.

"Is this the first time you've noticed?" Brand asked with a teasing glint in his eye.

Ember snorted and whacked his backside with the tip of her tail. It was a method of discipline that worked well on hatchlings — as she could testify from personal experience — but to a nearly full-grown Scout dragon with scales, it was akin to the tickle of tuff-grass on belly skin. The next thing she knew Brand had landed heavily on her, his teeth groping for her throat. She heaved. He stuck. She rolled and he went with her. After a great deal of struggle and a lot more noise, they fell apart, laughing and gasping for breath.

Suddenly a tiny figure dashed across the ground and flung itself into the play fight, pounding against Brand's chest with puny fists and howling in childish ferocity. Brand blinked in surprise, then suddenly caught on and began to wail and beg for mercy. Prince Shadrel battered harder and bawled louder. Brand responded with equal vigor.

Yemah peered up from the strange object in his hands, rolled his eyes skyward, then returned to his work. Ember's curiosity finally got the best of her.

"What is it?" she asked, peering at the small dark object.

"It's called a compass," Yemah replied. "This needle always points towards the north, making it a simple matter to figure out what direction to take. With this, we're sure never to lose our way."

"It's magic, then?" she asked.

"Of a kind."

"Did your skilled magicians make it?"

Yemah shook his head. "We have no skilled magicians, only craftsmen. The needle is attracted by the force of the ground, and always points in the same direction. I helped make this compass myself, out of metals I took from the ground. My people excel at this art. We make these and many other useful items to trade with other people for the things we need."

Ember wasn't surprised, for she knew that this was one of the ways humans interacted with each other. Deciding that now was the time to bring up something else on her mind, she said, "May I ask you a more personal question?"

Yemah shrugged. "Go ahead, but I can't guarantee that I'll answer."

She took a deep breath. "How did your people meet Cidrok? You have to admit it's quite unusual for humans to befriend a dragon."

"I agree," he admitted, turning the compass around and squinting at it. "But we have always thought highly of dragons. When Cidrok arrived on our mountain, ill to the point of death, we didn't hesitate. We did everything we could to save him and we've made it our task to take care of him ever since. He is, after all, a unique dragon."

Ember was too surprised at this news to speak. As she hesitated, the time for questions vanished.

Yemah beckoned to Brand and Shadrel. "We need to rest for a short time," he announced to them all. "Then we'll begin our journey across the Great Sea. I've crossed it a few times, but never on the back of a dragon. The Great Sea is very unpredictable, prone to high winds and sudden storms. In boats it's a dangerous and risky business, even for a skillful sailor. I expect it to be even harder for us."

He paused, shuddered and stared out across the water, as if his own words had dredged up some unbearable memory. Ember never discovered what that memory might have been, for the next moment Yemah had turned away and was back doing what he did best: getting things organized.

Yemah insisted that they begin the crossing with full stomachs and Ember obeyed, even though eating was the last thing she felt like doing. Afterward she stretched out on the sand to let her dinner settle. The lap of the water upon the shore soothed her like a brood mother's song. The moons rose, silver-brilliant in the sky, casting shadows upon the rolling waves. She breathed in deeply, tasting the salty dampness of the air. Then Yemah called for them to rise. He came to her first and cinched the girth tightly beneath her belly. When he was done heaping bags upon her back, he turned to Brand.

"Are you ready for us to mount?"

"As ready as I'll ever be."

The jackdaws fluttered like moths around them as they rose into the night.

Chapter 8

The wind bore them along, strong enough to provide lift yet not so powerful as to drag them off their course. Moonlight dazzled over water; skuas encircled them like silver leaves adrift. As the hours slid by, Ember realized that her body was finally starting to adapt to the rigorous schedule of the last few days. Exertions that once exhausted her to the point of collapse now made her only moderately weary. As her muscles had firmed up, she had noticed her body becoming slimmer in some places and thicker in others. She had always known sooner or later she would lose the round belly of hatchlinghood and grow broader in the chest and rump, as did all maturing female dragons. What she hadn't expected was for it to happen quite so suddenly.

If Brand noticed, he didn't say. He seemed preoccupied with something. Ember had observed that he wasn't eating much, and he appeared to have lost some weight. He reminded her now of a huge damselfly — all gangly legs and gauzy wings — topped off by a gaunt, hollow-eyed face.

It was sometime in the early hours of morning when Brand fell back beside her to inform her of Yemah's request.

"We need to stop for a rest!" he called above the wind's roar.

Ember peered down at the endless blue expanse below. "Where are we going to land?" she asked. "Do you see something I don't?"

"Cidrok recommended that we call up a humpback serpent from the ocean depths," Brand informed her.

Ember felt icy claws run down her spine. The scales on her back lifted in alarm.

"How is that done? And even if we succeed, who's to say it won't make a meal of us the first chance it gets?"

"It's either that," Brand replied, "or fly till we're

too tired to stay aloft. It won't take long to drown once that happens."

Ember could see his point. "All right, tell me what to do."

Cidrok had assured Brand that it would be a simple process. Apparently sea serpents, being distant cousins of the land-dwelling dragons, were able to speak the dragon language or maybe even the Common Tongue — he hadn't been sure which. Brand admitted he was nervous, but he was confident that Cidrok's wisdom was reliable.

"You have a lot of faith in him," Ember observed.

They sent out a call together, howling loud enough, Ember was certain, to rouse the locusts from their sandbeds. Another call. And another.

"How much longer?" she groaned.

Brand's reply was lost as a great, scale-raising bawl filled their ears. Ember lurched; her body spasmed in alarm. The sound screamed all around them like a cry of death. On it went, and higher it climbed, until Ember's head throbbed in protest and she feared it would surely split in two. Flowers of light bloomed before her eyes, and then it was over.

"We've made contact," Brand announced, proudly stating the obvious.

"I realize that," Ember growled, fighting nausea and a stabbing pain in the head.

"I can see him now. He's coming up on us fast," Brand commented. "He seems agitated. Cidrok did warn me that humpbacks can be temperamental."

"Where is he now?" Ember wondered aloud, peering over the waves.

"He went down again," Brand said.

They hovered, waiting. A few moments later the ocean parted beneath them, and up from its vast, murky-black depths rose the most gigantic humpback sea serpent she had ever seen. Never mind that it was the only humpback sea serpent she had ever seen; nothing that lived could possibly be larger than this. Ember wondered if she would die quickly in one great crunch, or slowly sizzle to an acidic end inside the monster's stomach.

"I knew it!" boomed the humpback serpent, with a voice like waves crashing on rocks. "Such a foul reek of flesh can only mean one thing. Dragons!"

Well, that was one little mystery solved. The serpent spoke a slightly garbled version of the Common Tongue. Something else. Ember had heard that humpback sea serpents had such powerful voices they could deafen a dragon with a single cry. But since so few dragons had made contact and lived to tell the tale, the story had never been confirmed. So mystery number two had been solved as well.

I'll be happy to let everyone know that it's true, Ember thought, if only I can make it through this in one piece.

"Great serpent of the deep!" cried Yemah. "We beg you to help us on our journey!"

"What is that little sea-worm prattling about?" the monster thundered. "Is it he who has disturbed the sleep of Hafen, the mighty serpent?"

"No, that was us," admitted Brand, lowering himself dangerously close to the waves. "But we intended no harm. We were instructed to call for you."

"By whom?"

"Cidrok."

"What? Cidrok! That most vile and despicable of dragons! Has no one told that overgrown slug to tend to his own affairs and leave me to mine?"

The serpent thrashed and heaved below; water churned and boiled, deluging them with spray. His shrieks of anger stabbed through Ember's battered brain and curled her claws. Then beyond the din she became aware of a tiny sound that pricked her throbbing senses like a thorn. A thin, high cry of pain. Prince Shadrel was crying.

"Stop, great serpent!" Yemah shouted, clutching Shadrel to his breast. "You don't know your own strength!"

"Quit it, you lout!" cried Brand. "If we chose, we could snap your bones like driftwood!"

What was he talking about? Ember wondered. That was the most ridiculous bluff she'd ever heard. The creature wouldn't fall for that one in a million cycles.

She hovered and watched as the serpent flopped and twisted below them, as if he was struggling mightily against some unseen danger. Suddenly, to her amazement, the tumult ceased as instantly as it had begun. The waves sloshed up and down, then gradually settled into place. The monster lay still in the dark water like the broken hull of some ancient manship. Shadrel's crying softened, then ended with a few sniffs and a series of small hiccups. For a moment Ember thought she saw a glimmer of magic, but then it was gone.

Yemah patted the child's head and spoke to Brand. "What's he doing now?"

"It's going to be all right," replied Brand. "Look."

The serpent had risen fully to the surface and was waiting with apparent patience for them to land on his back. Ember couldn't help but think that a volcano on the verge of erupting would be a safer place.

"How did you know?" Ember asked Brand under her breath.

"I didn't, really," he replied, just as quietly. "Maybe this sea serpent is just a big bully — all spray and no steam."

"How do we know the big bully won't strike again — and turn us into a tasty treat?"

"Let's just hope he's a coward. We don't have much choice, do we?"

Ember nodded in agreement, not feeling any better. "Yes, let's hope your threats are enough to keep us alive," she said.

Slowly descending, they set down on a mound of flesh the size of Cidrok's mountain.

Ember was astonished to discover that the serpent's skin, although wet, was not as slippery as it looked, and was faintly warm to the touch. So much for the myth of the cold and slimy sea monster, she thought to herself. Too bad his personality wasn't as pleasantly surprising.

They took turns sleeping and watching while the serpent plowed steadily and silently southward at a rapid pace. Ember slept, then woke to a sky gray and heavy with unfallen rain. Shadrel, despite a long leash tethering him to a saddle strap, was making a game of rolling to and fro across the monster's back. His laughter broke like bubbles in the hazy air. Yemah sat stiff and silent, staring at the black and baleful sea and the glowering sky.

Brand suddenly jerked upright, and spoke: "Someone is coming. We've got to leave!"

Ember scrambled to her feet. "What do you — " She never finished, for all at once Yemah let out a ghastly yell and half staggered, half slid across the serpent's back toward them.

"Pack up!" he howled, scrambling for bags and boy, his eyes flashing white in their sockets. Beside her, Ember heard the hissing intake of Brand's breath and followed his gaze upwards to the northeast.

They were still far off, hardly larger than a splatter of freckles across the pallid skin of sky. But they were flying in the right formation and moving at the right speed to be none other than a herd of Hunting dragons. And Ember had no doubts about who they were and what their intended quarry might be.

Thankfully Yemah hadn't removed the saddles from their backs. Ember felt the bags land with a sharp thump against her spine. Yemah grabbed Shadrel in his arms and dashed toward Brand, who knelt to receive them. The human grabbed the

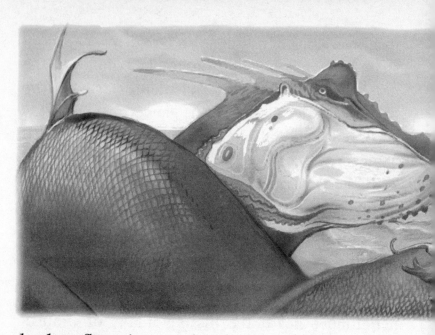

leather flaps in one hand and with the other heaved himself and Shadrel up.

The next moment Hafen dived.

What saved them was the serpent's enormous size, which made it impossible for him to slip cleanly and instantly into the sea. In those few precious seconds of warning — as the water churned and swelled beside the monster's sinking body — Ember and Brand lifted frantically skyward, Ember with the bags slung carelessly over her back and Brand with the two humans dangling, half mounted, over the boiling froth.

They skimmed with desperate speed across the pitching sea. Ember's muscles throbbed and her

breath came in ragged hisses, but the effort was in vain. The pursuing dragons loomed closer and closer. It hardly surprised her, for the herd carried no riders or supplies and was made up entirely of full-grown Scout dragons at the peak of their prowess and strength. Herd Father's hunting group would contain no less than the best. Weaklings did not last long with Father. It was interesting to Ember that he had brought his entire ensemble just to catch two undersized adolescents, a human child, and a stick of a man. But then, Herd Father had never been one to take insult gracefully.

The attack, when it finally came, was much worse than Ember had anticipated. Herd Father swooped down upon Brand, who swerved to protect his riders from the deadly teeth and claws. Shadrel and Yemah were instantly unseated, the tether snapped, and they plunged downward to disappear beneath the angry swell. The next moment Brand took the full brunt of Father's hit. The sound made by the impact of their bodies would have shattered stone. Brand tumbled through the air, miraculously recovered, and turned back toward his attacker.

"I should have killed you the moment you crawled from your shell!" thundered Herd Father. "When I saw your red scales I knew it would eventually come to this! You're a traitor — born from a long line of traitors!"

"What stopped you?" roared Brand as he skimmed past, snapping and clawing. A gout of orange flame hissed from Herd Father's jaws and would have set Brand's wings on fire had he not been so nimble.

"The herd mothers talked me out of it," he bellowed. "It's a mistake I will soon remedy."

"Not if I can help it!" Brand cried. He was a crimson predator with wings, all teeth and claws and spitting flame, as he spun in dizzy circles over, around, and under the larger dragon.

Ember banked violently to avoid a spew of fire

from a beefy blue dragon on her tail and noticed two bedraggled heads bobbing directly below her in the sea. Relief coursed through her veins. The next instant she froze in helpless horror as Hafen's vicious, gaping jaws rose above the surface to engulf boy, man, and all the water that surrounded them. Then he was gone, back to the evil, squalid depths he had come from.

Ember's gaze flashed back to Brand in time to see one of Herd Father's hind claws rake a scarlet stripe down his belly from chest to flank. The blood fell down like rain. The battle had finally turned in the herd's favor, and when the dragon behind her caught up at last she gave in without a fight, folded her wings, and plunged headlong into the churning brine.

CHAPTER 9

Ember thought it would take less time to die. If she had drowned immediately, as she had expected, she wouldn't have known the difference. But now here she was, drifting slowly downward like a fish that had swallowed a stone, fully conscious and wanting very much to live.

It was painfully obvious that she had to go up instead of down. With that in mind, she spread her wings and kicked. Immediately she found herself careening wildly to one side. Several tries later she started to panic. The best she could do, apparently, was hold herself in place, but already her chest ached and little red lights sparkled in front of her eyes. She flapped and flailed in terror. The churning water dragged at her limbs like thick muck. Instinctively she opened her mouth to scream and only gagged as water rushed in to fill her nose and throat.

"Quit thrashing, you fool!" an angry voice roared above her. "You are a fire-breathing dragon. Your body is full of excess oxygen. Dragons never drown from lack of air — only from gulping in too much water! Now calm down until I reach you!"

It was Hafen — coming to devour her, no doubt. Why didn't he just let her die peacefully, and then eat her at his leisure? Most likely he preferred his meat still kicking as it went down. She relaxed. A cool calmness filled her brain. She could slash his vile throat wide open with her claws as she slid on through. But she couldn't allow him to see a single flicker of movement, for success would depend upon complete surprise. She hung in the water, her heart thudding.

He drew near; the water swelled and darkened around her as he moved beneath. She found herself pinned flat against his back by the crushing weight of the ocean as he shoved her roughly upward toward the air and light.

"I have no intention of eating you," the serpent growled as they surfaced. "Dragons give me a stomach ache and terrible amounts of gas. I wouldn't swallow one if it fell into my mouth."

Ember sucked in air — sweet, delicious, glorious air — and let it out in one great spasm of coughing. As she clung to his back, Hafen twisted his great head fully around, exposing his neck. Foolish serpent! Now he would pay for the deaths of her friends! She lunged for his throat, tripped, and rolled snout-over-tail across his back to slam against the hump. What little breath she had managed to recover hissed from her lungs in an undignified whoop. She struggled to rise. Weakness struck like a blow.

"Idiot," Hafen snarled. "You're even dumber than I thought."

His vast jaws gaped wide open as they turned toward her again. She gathered what remaining strength she possessed and waited. Hafen's neck twisted and his body shuddered as if he was being guided by a will greater than his own. Nearer the jaws came, and nearer. Her body trembled; her muscles tensed for what would certainly be her final chance.

The next moment Yemah and Shadrel tumbled from the serpent's mouth to land in a heap beneath her nose.

She jumped in sheer amazement; the serpent's

head swiveled upward and away.

Yemah and Shadrel rose upon shaky feet, wet with slime and reeking of seaweed and raw fish, but Ember hardly noticed. The boy leaped on her neck, winding his arms gleefully around her. The man patted her shoulder in a rough, almost embarrassed way and muttered something about being glad she was all right. The joy that thrilled through her veins came close to anguish.

"Where . . . what . . ." she managed to gasp.

"We were in the hump," replied Yemah with a shudder. "He kept air there for us, if you can call that foul, fetid brew air. Smelled like a dragon's feed pit at noonday, only ten times worse." He shuddered again.

Ember let the comment about feed pits go by.

"But why did he do it?" she asked. "It's obvious the serpent would just as soon gobble us down as cooperate. What I'd like to know is, who's stopping him?"

With a lurch Hafen surged forward, picking up speed. He wasn't wasting any time now. There was no doubt in Ember's mind that he was anxious to conclude the journey and be rid of them.

Yemah left Shadrel with her and scrambled to a higher point on Hafen's back. He peered in all directions, searching the sea and sky for any sign of movement.

"Brand is still alive," she assured him. "I'm sure I saw him a moment ago. Herd Father and the others seem to have backed off, but I can't figure out why. They had us beaten."

"Hafen drove them off," said Yemah impatiently. "Where did you say Brand was?"

"He's back there, just above the water."

"I see him now, but something's gone wrong," said Yemah.

Ember paused, worry flooding her mind.

It was true. Brand was coming in like a sea swan battered by a gale. From this distance and at this angle he looked like an untidy bundle of sticks. His flight path was jagged and skewed, and as he made his approach Ember saw that the red of his belly and legs were stained to a darker crimson by the blood that had seeped from his wounds.

He landed heavily on Hafen's back like a rock dropped from the sky and lay there in a tangle of wings and legs. Yemah scrambled toward him. Fear swelled in Ember's chest and rose like fire in her throat. After a few heart-thudding seconds Brand opened one eye and gasped, "Not one of my better landings."

No one laughed. They could see his condition was serious.

Yemah quickly backtracked in a desperate

search for something he seemed to have lost. It took Ember a moment to realize what was missing — the saddle and bags she had been carrying upon her back, the bags that had gone down with her during the attack. One glance told her that Brand's saddle, as well, had been lost in the battle.

"They're probably at the bottom of the Great Sea by now," she said sadly to Yemah.

The man ran frantic fingers through his mass of tangled hair. "The red dragon needs bandages and blankets or his body will go into shock!" he almost wailed.

Ember had heard about dragons going into shock but knew nothing of the treatment. What she did know — what her own brood mother had taught her from hatchlinghood — was that the first action to take with any wound is to lick it clean. She crawled over to where Brand lay and proceeded to do just that. His body was cold beneath her tongue.

Gradually the bleeding eased.

Yemah paced back and forth beside them.

"Something in your saliva is helping to clot the blood," he said, his voice still high and anxious. "But I'm worried about internal bleeding."

Ember stretched out full-length beside Brand's icy body and draped one wing over him to hold in what little heat remained. It was a highly awkward position, but she was past caring. She had more pressing matters than her own comfort to worry about.

Worrying about Hafen was a good place to start. The serpent was rude, sarcastic and downright nasty, and she didn't trust him as far as she could spit bones. It was true she knew nothing about magic and she had no idea how it worked, but even she could see that some kind of powerful spell was holding the humpback monster in check. At first she had admired the strength of Shadrel's mind and marveled at the power of one so young, but now she was beginning to wonder. Maybe Yemah hadn't lied to her, after all. She was starting to believe that she had things figured out all wrong. It was a vague feeling of unease — something she couldn't quite put a claw on — but the boy was too eager, too innocent, too inexperienced, and the serpent was much too strong to be so easily controlled.

This brought her to another worry.

Yemah might not have lied, but he was definitely withholding information. Ember wasn't sure exactly what it was he knew so much about, only that it was making him miserable and extra disagreeable, even for a human. And this, finally,

brought her to worry number three.

For the first time in all of the cycles she had known him, Brand had been keeping secrets from her. Now he was badly wounded, unconscious, lost to her. Suddenly a great slab of stone had rolled into place, and only emptiness remained.

She nuzzled Brand's snout and called his name, but the only indication of life she received was the shallow hiss of his breath and the shiver of his ravaged flesh against her own.

They traveled on. The worries remained; no answers came. The sun rose and set; they slept and wakened and slept again. Yemah and Prince Shadrel drank from the remaining waterskin. They shared fish from the sea, which Ember, for the child's sake, conceded to cook. The hours dragged by in endless monotony. Brand lay limp on the serpent's back, conscious but growing ever weaker. At last, when Ember felt for certain the Great Sea would indeed go on forever and they would surely perish beneath the relentless waves, she raised her head and saw a vast stretch of land lying dark and hazy against the far horizon.

CHAPTER 10

Ember stood on Hafen's back beside Brand and surveyed the shoreline that stretched out before them in a long, ragged line. She knew without being told that they had arrived at Kowtow, the land of humans, for she didn't have to look all that closely to see that the landscape here was vastly different from anything she had ever seen before.

Clumps of man-made structures were scattered across the rocky ground like warts. Smoke belched from holes in their tops, staining the sky a dirty grey and poisoning the wind with a bitter, acrid smell. Hills rose in the distance,

not in graceful peaked symmetry or capped in dazzling white, like the mountains in Callore, but in a
string of dull brown mounds.

Ember shivered. She turned toward Brand, who
was trying valiantly to stand on four limbs and
nearly succeeding. She found herself fearing that
the next wind gust would topple his wasted body
face first in the sea.

"At last we're here. But I don't know which is worse," she grumbled, "the serpent we just rode on or the land we're about to step on."

"Mmm-bah," said a tiny voice at her feet. Ember peered down, intrigued by Shadrel's attempt to speak her name in the Common Tongue. A moment later Yemah grabbed the boy and boosted him up onto her back. She had expected this; Brand lacked the strength to carry anything more than his own weight, if that. She felt the child land upon her rump and begin scrambling awkwardly toward the ridge of her spine. Then Yemah climbed on behind him and took a firm grasp of her scale-skin, for lack of anything else to hold onto. They were ready to go.

Hafen howled as they rose from his back and circled above him. His grey hump of body dwindled dizzily as they climbed. Kowtow spread out before them like a huge, dark scab. Wind whined in Ember's ears and tore at her wings. Brand faltered, drifted lower, struggled bravely to rise. She eased her pace to match his. Slowly, ever so slowly, they struggled nearer to the shore.

Then the rocky beach lay below them and after that came the lumpy, upward swelling of the hills.

The next moment Brand teetered like a wounded bird and began to spiral downward.

She watched in sick helplessness as he attempted to save himself. He fluttered, end over end, like a fragile, scarlet leaf tossed by an autumn wind. The thud of his body on the unyielding earth must have jarred his spine from neck to tip of tail and spasmed every muscle in his body.

It took all of the willpower Ember possessed not to dive in howling panic to the ground. Instead she forced herself to settle slowly earthward, every moment passing like an eon. As she landed, Brand's eyes rolled back in their sockets; then the lids fell shut. Yemah took Shadrel in his arms and scrambled from her back to the ground. And from somewhere out at sea came a howl that could have blasted Cidrok's mountain to dust.

The sea exploded. Skuas rose screaming into air. Waves lashed the shore, white with froth. The cry of fury that knifed through Ember's brain was beyond pain. It was Hafen's howl of violation — the cry of a creature who has been used against his will, a shriek of rage and resentment.

A sudden, awful thought flashed through Ember's mind. Had Brand been controlling Hafen all along — and now that he was unconscious, the sea serpent was free to vent his wrath? That would mean Shadrel was just an ordinary human boy, after all. But if Brand was the one with all the magic, where did he get it from? And why had Cidrok kept this vital information to himself? Why had Yemah not told her sooner? Why didn't Brand trust her?

Ember turned to confront Yemah. He could no longer deny the truth; the signs were so clear that even she could see it now.

But before she could speak Yemah dropped to his knees beside Brand's still form and began stroking the dragon's bruised snout. His body shook with sobs, and the tears dripped through the fur on his face onto the sand below. He howled into Brand's ear, then flopped down and wailed into the dirt. It was more than Ember could bear.

"Yemah," she said, choking down her own worry that Brand might die. "This isn't helping."

Shadrel's cry of fear joined with Yemah's.

"What's going on?" she cried above the clamor. "Tell me right now! I'm tired of not knowing what's going on!"

Yemah pushed himself up and looked at her with dull, red-rimmed eyes. He wiped his sodden face with one grimy sleeve, and said, "You're right. I should have told you sooner."

"Then why didn't you?" she hissed.

"The red dragon made me promise not to," Yemah mumbled. He reached for Shadrel and gathered the boy into his arms. The crying ceased.

Ember pressed on. "Something happened, when we were saving Shadrel from Herd Father, that made me believe he has magic. But he doesn't, does he?"

"No," Yemah sighed. "And yes."

Ember glared at him. "I'm getting tired of the riddles," she complained. "I'm no good at them and they just make me cross. I'll try a different question. Did Brand save us from the locusts?"

"Yes," came Yemah's bleak reply. "And no."

Ember suppressed the urge to scream in frustration. One look at Brand's broken body was all it took. "Did Brand force the serpent to help us?" she asked.

Yemah nodded. "Brand and Shadrel worked together to control the serpent and the locusts. Don't you see? That's the way it works. Dragons have magic, but they can't use it without the help of special humans called Dragon Lords. You thought we stole your magic, but that's not what happened at all. When your ancestors refused to live among humans, their magic became dormant. But it's still there inside of them — inside of you. Dragons and humans can only reach their full potential when they work together. That's the way it was in ancient times, and that's the way it will always be. At first I didn't believe it was happening, because Shadrel is so young and most Dragon Lords don't develop their skill at accessing a dragon's magic until they're in their teens. But then I remembered that Shadrel has always loved dragons. His mother descended from Dragon Lords, and so did his father. And then, of course, there's the prophecy."

"What prophecy?"

"The one that says a red dragon will someday restore all that his kind destroyed."

Ember shook her head, trying to clear the muddle. "Destroy? What did they destroy?"

"The red dragons were the ones who sided with the evil Lord Goran those hundreds of cycles ago."

"How do you learn these things? Did Cidrok tell you?"

Yemah nodded. "Yes, but it was nothing I didn't already know. My people have told stories about dragons and Dragon Lords for centuries."

"Oh? It's strange that you know more about us than we do. What other stories do you tell?"

Yemah either ignored the bite in her voice or was too disheartened to care.

"We believe that when the red dragons fly over Kowtow there will be peace among all creatures."

"Are there other red dragons?" Ember was surprised.

"We don't know, but we hope there are. Brand is the only one we've found so far. Cidrok sent me along to protect him, as well as to take care of Prince Shadrel. I have failed at this task, and because of my failure, my people and all humans and dragons everywhere will suffer."

She shook her head as she tried to think of a way to comfort him, and could not. Some comfort was what she herself could use right now.

Ember lowered her head. "You betrayed me, Brand," she said to the lifeless heap beside her. "I thought I knew you. I trusted you and followed you, and you paid me back with lies."

"Do you think that's fair, at a time like this?" Yemah asked.

Ember stared at the man, dumbfounded. Was this the man who, only minutes earlier, had been sobbing and rolling around in the dirt like a mad-man?

"Brand didn't betray you. He's only beginning to realize what he is and all that it means," said Yemah.

"I was the best friend he ever had," she said in an attempt to defend her position. "He should have trusted me." She paused and tried to think through her feelings rationally.

"Maybe it's not too late to save him," Yemah

said suddenly. "You fly for help. I'll stay here and watch him and Shadrel. Hurry!"

"Where should I go?" she asked.

If she had known he would send her to the largest city in Kowtow, to the centre of human commerce and civilization, to the castle of the King of Kowtow himself, where humans would be thick as mud-tics on a zebu's hide, she'd have fled from Cidrok's cave long ago when she still had the chance. But now it was a matter of life and death, and her fear of men was small compared to everything else at stake. She had to save Brand no matter what it took.

Yemah drew a maze of lines in the dirt with his finger and explained where to go. It was clear to him, but made little sense to her. She decided she'd simply have to trust him, set a straight course in the direction he indicated, and hope for the best. She spread her wings and rose into the sooty sky. The last thing she saw as the landscape spun away beneath her was the boy prince, now shrunk to the size of a gigbeetle, running back and forth across the sand and calling out her name.

CHAPTER 11

Ember, having navigated alone through the range of hills and beyond, was now approaching what appeared to be the city of the King of Kowtow. The king's castle, from the air at least, looked like the result of a small avalanche. It was built of black stone, and jutted out at odd angles — whether by design or accident, she wasn't sure.

The surrounding district wasn't any more attractive. Dull, decrepit houses leaned into the alleyways. The air hung thick and gray over the streets, especially where smoke billowed from ugly towers that reached like dirty foreclaws to the sky. It was beyond her wildest imaginings that she was flying open-eyed into the exact situation she had spent her entire life trying to avoid.

Ember circled the castle once, then twice, before finally coming to rest nearby upon a flat stone surface within a circle of water. She wondered how long it would take the castle's occupants to realize a dragon had landed in their midst. As it turned out, not long at all.

She had hardly caught her breath when a battered door opened to disgorge a stream of humans. Seeing her, they milled in confusion around the entrance, pointing and chattering in the meaningless gabble they called language. She waited, shuddering inwardly and wondering when someone would arrive to take charge. *If you don't survive, Brand,* she thought to herself, *and I've done all of this for nothing, I'll leave the prickleweeds to thrive upon your miserable grave.*

Still she waited, and was finally rewarded when a striking figure strode through the open doorway. The crowd parted to let him pass. As he drew close, Ember saw that he was taller than the others. He wore boots and several layers of colorful false skin, a sure sign of his importance. He stopped and studied her, calmly assessing the situation. In a few moments he seemed to arrive at a decision and

turned, motioning toward the crowd.

"Fiske!"

A small, neat human scuttled from the group and knelt in front of him. Ember guessed that the tall man must be the King of Kowtow, for he carried an air of authority. The king spoke to the little man, who nodded and then turned toward her.

"Great lady dragon," Fiske began, in a surprisingly good rendition of the Common Tongue. Then his fear got the better of him. He trembled and backed away. The poor fellow didn't take more than two steps before the king moved in to block his retreat.

It was plain to see that he was as uncomfortable with dragons as she had always been with humans. At least until a few moments ago. Now, as she gazed around at all the wide eyes and startled faces, she had trouble finding much to be afraid of. The irony of the situation almost made her laugh out loud. Slowly she lowered her snout to appear less threatening and said, "Yes, brave human, I'm listening."

Fiske looked up in near horror. "G–g–great l–lady d–d–dragon," he began again, "the k–king wonders what has b–b–brought you to our land."

Now was her chance. She just hoped he could get the story straight when he reported to the king.

"I've come from far away, seeking safety for the human prince, Shadrel. I've brought with me a mountain man named Yemah and the dragon, Brand. My companions are waiting by the sea. The dragon is severely wounded. We need your help."

Fiske stared at her with his mouth agape, then turned and began explaining to the king.

But the king had understood her well enough, and with a thump of boots and a swirl of green false skin he disappeared back into the castle. His spokesman scuttled after him. Unfortunately, the rest of the group didn't follow, but remained behind to stare curiously at Ember and to whisper among themselves.

Ember smiled to herself at her new-found peace. She realized she no longer felt any hatred towards the humans. In fact, she almost liked them; they were such curious little creatures. She thought she might as well entertain them while she was waiting. Filling her lungs, she sent a healthy blast of fire into the air above their heads. At once they scrambled for the door, practically flattening one another in their haste to get away.

She watched with amusement until they were gone, then stretched out on the cobblestones and closed her eyes. Might as well relax, she decided. Nothing I can do now but wait. Her stomach rumbled, reminding her of how long she'd gone without food or water. She wondered if they would think to offer her something to eat . . .

~ ~ ~ ~ ~ ~ ~ ~ ~ ~ ~ ~

As it turned out, her hosts had thought of that and more. She woke to the sound of Fiske's voice whining in her ears.

"Lady dragon," he called from a safe distance, "you must wake up and eat! You are leaving shortly!"

Ember's eyes flew open. Food and water had been placed in bowls beside her. A makeshift saddle lay nearby.

She gulped down water between mouthfuls of human food that was cooked dry but still delicious. Brood Mother would have slapped her on the snout for her poor manners, but she had never been so hungry in her life. The journey had been harder on her than she had realized.

"My king wants to know if you will carry two riders," Fiske said.

"It's nothing I haven't already done," she said when she finally raised her head. "Is one of the riders to be you?"

He appeared horrified at the thought. "No, no, lady dragon," he quickly assured her. "Just the physician, Licea — and a visitor to our palace named King Briais. My own king and the rest of his men have started out with horses and a wagon."

Ember stiffened in surprise at the mention of Shadrel's father's name.

Fiske took a deep breath and continued. "You have to hurry. The Horde has moved close to our city. Your friends are in terrible danger."

"The Horde?"

"Our enemies — the desert people. Recently they invaded our land. They landed in huge ships. They raided the farmers' crops, robbed our merchants, and burned our property. They are growing stronger, and seek to dethrone our king and rule in his place. It is a sad state of affairs that you find us in."

"I understand completely," Ember muttered into her meal. "I've had some experience with The Horde myself." Her heart sank. Cidrok had thought that Shadrel would be safe in Kowtow — but the trouble had spread.

"Pardon, lady dragon?"

She was saved from repeating herself by the arrival of two more humans. At first Ember didn't pay much attention to the second human, so entranced was she with the first. As his large, dark eyes gazed kindly upon her, she was reminded of the large, dark eyes of Shadrel, the prince.

"Thank you, young dragon," King Briais said, in a strong yet gentle voice. "Thank you for saving my son."

She stared at him in stunned silence, not knowing what to say. Then she glanced at his companion.

The physician was a female. This, in itself, was not surprising to Ember, for she came from a herd where the oldest brood mother was also the herd healer. But what did give her a jolt was seeing a human female up close for the first time. It caught her unprepared. This human was smaller and more slender than the males of her kind, with a mane of yellow fur that sprang from her head and fell all the way down her back to her waist. But she was obviously no weakling. She stood straight and firm, and the eyes that met Ember's were clear and bright with confidence.

While Fiske placed the saddle on Ember's back, King Briais paused at her head and raised his hand to her snout. In an almost absent-minded way, his fingers traveled down to her throat where the scales were softer, and gently stroked her skin.

The unfamiliar contact was a shock, but Ember had to admit it felt good. Then, reminding herself

that this was a man who knew and understood
dragons — their weaknesses as well as their
strengths — she quickly pulled away. Even though
she had heard only good things said of him, trusting humans was a new thing for her. It would be
wise to hold back until she knew him better.

As he and Licea prepared to mount, Ember
glanced upward and noticed four griffins circling
in the sky overhead.

In Callore griffins had long been extinct. The

huge lion-birds were scavengers by nature. The trouble began when they suddenly developed a taste for newly laid dragon eggs and took to raiding nests. The battle was long and brutal, but the dragons were fighting for the lives of their offspring and would not back down. In the end all of the griffins were driven from Callore.

Ember had never seen a live griffin, but there was no mistaking them. Rare, intelligent, and aglow with magic, to her they were the most amazing creatures imaginable. She watched their antics with wonder and delight.

"Where are they from?" she asked Fiske, who was tightening the saddle straps in readiness for takeoff. "Are they coming with us?"

"These are the king's griffins," he explained, nodding in answer to her question. "In Kowtow, griffins are trained to protect the king and his guests."

She was surprised anew. What kept such glorious creatures in servitude to mere humans? She shook her head in puzzlement, but only for a moment. King Briais and Licea had mounted and were ready to go. Ember unfolded her wings and rose into the sunless sky, the squad of griffins slowly circling around her.

CHAPTER 12

The low brown hills were almost behind them when Ember heard the hoofbeats. She had flown low and fast, making good time and feeling relieved that this would soon be over. The sun had even managed to slip a few feeble rays through the sludgy sky to lift her spirits and carry her along. Then she heard what sounded like galloping windmounts below.

She knew it couldn't mean anything good. A moment later her fear was confirmed. Her long-range vision revealed that a small group of mounted desert men had almost reached the spot where

Shadrel and Yemah waited beside Brand's unconscious body.

The sight of them sent a surge of panic through her veins. She lurched wildly in the air and would have unseated both riders but for their firm hold on the saddle. She recovered and offered a meek apology in the Common Tongue, but they were too preoccupied to reply.

Fear drove her to fly even faster.

"Ember," King Briais called to her above the wind. "Has my son been captured? Tell me what you see."

"Yes, great king," she cried. "The Horde have spotted Yemah and Shadrel and will soon carry them away."

When he spoke, she barely recognized his voice. Filled with outrage, it rumbled in her head like tumbling stones. "Fly as low as you can," he commanded her. "Follow the valley, skim between the trees. Don't worry about the griffins — they'll follow our lead. We have the advantage of surprise. Let's use it!"

She obeyed, flying as quickly and silently as she could. If not for the throbbing of her heart in her ears and the singing of the wind upon her wings, the silence would have been complete.

She had never pushed herself this hard before. It

wasn't the distance that taxed her so greatly but the speed at which she travelled and the fact that she'd just swallowed enough food to give her a week-long stomach burn. King Briais urged her faster yet. She willed her muscles to comply. Up they went and over a ridge, down through a clump of trees that nearly cleaned off the tips of her wings, then along a narrow river bottom. She lost her sense of direction when she flew this close to the ground, and could only follow where he directed and hope for the best. The river bottom came to a sudden end as the river spilled sharply down toward the sea. She plunged after it, so close she could have dipped her snout in the water.

A moment later Ember realized they were there. She hardly had time to gulp down the terror that rose in her throat before they descended nosefirst on the cluster of humans.

"Spit fire, my young dragon," King Briais commanded her. "Singe a few furry eyebrows!"

And then, without another word, both he and Licea rolled from her back into the enemy's midst.

As she hurtled past, she saw the king unseat his first soldier and leap onto the windmount's back. She swung in a tight circle without slowing and spewed fire in one great orange arc. Men shouted. Windmounts whinnied and reared, their eyes rolling. She whirled back. New circle, new spout of flame. Circle, flame. Circle, flame.

Then the griffins struck.

Their battle tactic was simple. They flew low with their beaks open and their talons extended, slashing a pathway through the crowd toward Yemah, Shadrel and Brand. Their size, the flap of their enormous wings, and the nerve-rattling cries that accompanied the attack must have appeared formidable from below. Now and then one of the griffins would pluck up a man, carry him for a few seconds and drop him, kicking and yelling, down upon his fellows.

The skirmish was over almost before it began. This being only a small contingent of the main Horde army, they must have decided that two prisoners and a half-dead dragon weren't worth the risk. A short time later, they had retreated back toward the coast.

Ember landed heavily near Brand and watched as King Briais cut the ropes from Prince Shadrel and clutched the boy joyfully to his breast. Licea stumbled across the broken ground to free Yemah and together they rushed to Brand's side.

"We did our best," Ember whispered to her unconscious friend. "Don't let it be for nothing."

Knowing she could do no more, she left Brand

in Licea's care and returned to the air to keep watch. Circle and search. Circle and search. It seemed that, at least for the present, they were alone. Off to the northwest she saw the soldiers rejoining the main body of their army. But what she also saw to the south, which The Horde could not, was the King of Kowtow and his troops astride their horses, drawing rapidly closer. The battle would take place after she and her comrades were gone.

She watched as a massive wagon rattled to a halt beside Brand's lifeless body. The men worked together to roll him onto a large false skin and drag him up the ramp. At last they had him loaded on the wagon. With Licea and Yemah watching over him, they headed back toward the castle as quickly as the horses could take them.

Shadrel and King Briais were left to return with her. The boy wouldn't let go of his father's neck, even to mount, but the king was too happy to care. He just laughed and held his son all the more tightly as they scrambled up her side and into the saddle.

At last they were ready. Ember lifted skyward to follow the griffins' lead and a strange tingle of pride rippled through her. She carried King Briais — a true friend of dragons — and his son, the Prince of Callore, on her back.

CHAPTER 13

Brand was dying. Two days had passed, two long days in Kowtow. Ember lay on the castle balcony in the darkness, listening to his breathing grow weaker and fainter with every passing hour.

The physician Licea had done everything in her power.

"I've repaired the damaged organs," she had explained to Ember, rubbing her hand across her weary brow. "I've stopped the internal bleeding and stitched up the deepest lacerations."

To Ember the physician had looked as if she'd been dragged through the heart of Dark Forest and back again.

Lines etched her pale face and purple smudges stained the skin beneath her swollen eyes.

She had continued. "This is only the second time I've done surgery on a dragon. It was very complicated and a little frightening. However, the operation was successful, the wounds are healing and I see no reason why he won't recover."

But he hadn't recovered, and everyone in the castle was worried to distraction. Yemah had worked himself into such a state of frenzy and self-blame that Ember finally got fed up with the whining and snivelling and sent him scurrying from the room. Shadrel proved to be less noisy but no less annoying. He kept returning to the room bearing gifts for Brand — a muddy stick, three black rocks and something that had once been worn on a woman's foot. Thankfully that was the end of it; however the offending objects remained. Now Ember lay alone, unable to sleep, wondering what, if anything, could be done.

Then it came to her. As she hovered on the verge of sleep, a flash of insight snapped her instantly back to wakefulness.

Brand had told her once that he knew when she was dreaming about the humans, and that he had experienced it with her. Yemah had explained that Brand possessed magic, just as all dragons did. Just as she did. Perhaps she could use some of that magic now. Perhaps the same magic that allowed Brand to enter her dream would let her go into his.

Among dragons, something like this had never been discussed. Indeed, she hadn't known that dragons still had magic. She had no idea where to begin, but she knew she had to try. These were desperate and unusual circumstances. This was a matter of life and death.

Ember stretched out, relaxed, and focused all of her thoughts on Brand.

At first nothing happened. Then came a strange kind of darkness that filled her mind. She tried to move through it, but the effort reminded her of flying through a dense fog. It seemed to take forever. Finally she felt herself slipping into a hazy sleep and at last, into Brand's place of dreams.

Brand rested in a sunlit, flower-strewn meadow beside heaps of harvested cone-nuts, vines laden with fresh fruit, piles of freshly roasted meat — and dragons. There was a herd father (a much kinder-looking version), several brood mothers (the fat and cheerful variety), and more hatchlings than she could number. They were all waiting in eager adulation upon Brand, and they all looked exactly like him. Ember had never seen so much red all in one place. It was enough to make her eyes sore.

She moved as close to Brand as she could get without tromping on hatchling clawnails, and raised her snout to his.

"You lied to me, Brand," she said bluntly. The anger, which she had thought was gone, billowed up anew.

His eyes slowly focused. He groaned. "Which time?" he muttered.

Ember wasn't amused. She felt the heat of her frustration rising higher. Her words lashed out like flame.

"You told me it was Shadrel who used magic on The Horde, sent away the locusts, and — "

"I didn't say that. You drew your own conclusions."

"You deceived me."

He sighed, turning away. "I admit it. Now go and let me be."

Brand was losing his concentration. Several of the little red hatchlings popped out of existence.

"I will if you answer one last question," she growled.

"Fine, then, if it will make you leave."

"Why didn't you tell me about the magic?"

With that his face took on a sort of pained look, as though she had just cleared her nose in his food pile. She thought he might not answer after all, but

finally the words came.

"I didn't realize it myself at first. When Herd Father went for Shadrel, the boy screamed and everything happened at once. I felt something tingling inside, but I didn't understand what it meant. Shadrel's use of my magic was so uncontrolled it shot over everyone. Later, I felt the magic growing inside of me and I realized that somehow Shadrel was directing it. After that I started to remember."

"Remember?"

"Back at the cave, Cidrok dropped a few hints."

"Of course," she groaned. "A few hints. It

wouldn't do for him to tell you outright. That would be too easy."

"You should learn to trust in Cidrok's wisdom."

"Trust?" she guffawed. "Look who's speaking of trust! When you learned this about yourself, why didn't you tell me?"

"*One* last question, remember?"

"This is still part of the same question."

She knew she was making progress when he chuckled in spite of himself. One of the brood mothers and half of the food pile faded into oblivion.

"I was waiting," Brand said. "You were still

struggling to overcome your prejudice against humans, and you needed time. But then time ran out."

"That's a sorry excuse," she said.

"It's not an excuse," Brand said with exaggerated care. "There's more. You know I was born a Scout dragon, and I'll be a Scout dragon all of my life. That can never change. You and I have always been good friends, but we can never be anything more. I can never be your mate. And now you have lost your family because of this mission to save Shadrel. But I have the chance to fix that. If I die, it will help you. You can return to your herd and blame everything on me. You will belong, once again, to them."

"But I need you, Brand!" she cried. "I don't need them. I don't belong there anymore."

"She's right, Brand," said a voice. "You have a lot to live for."

King Briais stood tall and regal among the hatchlings, smack in the centre of Brand's dream. Ember couldn't believe what she was seeing. She blinked and shook her head but the king remained where he was. She had never heard of anything like this in the dragon stories of Callore. But then Brand was no ordinary dragon, and Briais was no ordinary king.

"Please leave me alone, Dragon Lord," Brand

groaned, covering his face with one wing. "Can't a sick and sorry dragon be left to perish in peace?"

"Brand," the king said gravely, "All of Callore needs you, for you and others like you are our only hope for peace. Now is not the time for you to die, for more than one reason. Your own father is yet alive."

Ember gasped. Brand's head snapped up. King Briais continued in that the same serious manner. "Cidrok told you of my lifelong friend, the dragon with the missing claw. What Cidrok didn't tell you is that he is a red dragon like you. His name is Skortch. He is your father."

Brand was too stunned to speak.

Ember muttered under her breath. "I wonder what else Cidrok forgot to mention?"

"Skortch's herd was killed by other dragons — dragons who feared and hated him for his color. Because red dragons helped cause that terrible war, many of your kind will never trust them again. But they forget that the legends say red dragons will someday bring peace to this land and help restore the rule of the Dragon Lords.

"Brand, you have to live. You're Skortch's only surviving offspring. And although your father is not here with us right now, I know he'd want his only son to live."

The remaining food, flowers, and hatchlings vanished in a puff of light. The next moment Ember found herself lying on the balcony of the King of Kowtow's ruin of a castle, staring dumbly up at Brand, who had just leaped fiercely from his sickbed. His eyes were blazing.

"Be careful," she warned him. "You're too weak to be up."

Brand's cry echoed from the turrets above. "Just let me go — to my father!"

Then he toppled to the floor in a heap.

CHAPTER 14

In spite of his good intentions, Brand was not able to move from the castle for more than a week. As he rested and recovered, King Briais took time to fill both of them in on the whole sad history of Brand's herd.

As the cycles passed, King Briais's connection with the dragon Skortch had continued to grow deeper and stronger. Eventually they learned to speak to each other without words, and when one of them was in danger, the other would always sense it. Then the time came when King Briais realized Skortch had magic, and that he, Briais, had the ability to use it. But they kept this a secret, for fear of what might happen if others found out.

Skortch grew into a Father and desired to establish a herd of his own. This he did. But his former herdmates, none of whom were red dragons, grew more and more alarmed at his alliance with the human enemy. Even though they didn't know the unfortunate history of red dragons, they did know that Skortch was different. They feared that his unhealthy friendship with a human would spread weakness like poison, and in the end destroy all of dragonkind. What they did next was, in their opinion, a matter of the survival of their entire species.

They attacked.

So not only was Skortch's newly established herd destroyed by dragons, it was destroyed by Skortch's own brothers, sisters, father and mothers. It was said, at the bitter, bloody end, that a great black dragon — with wings that spanned the sky like clouds of thunder and a scream that rocked the heavens — descended to clutch the bloodied, broken Skortch in his claws and carry him away.

King Briais concluded his story by saying that sometime during the terrible days that followed, Ember's herd discovered Brand's egg among the wreckage and ruin of what was left behind. Thankfully, he had been found by a herd less hostile than some others, and he was allowed to live and grow.

"Thank you, Brood Mother," Ember said to herself. "Thank all of you."

~ ~ ~ ~ ~ ~ ~ ~ ~ ~ ~ ~ ~ ~

The days passed and Brand gradually regained his strength, moving about the large gardens behind the castle. By the time he was fully recovered, he had confided to Ember that what he wanted most now was to go in search of his father.

"Since I'm meant to work for peace," Brand said, "that would be the best place to start."

"We will have to endure a lecture from Cidrok," Ember sighed. "He'd be insulted right to the tips of his clawnails if we flew over without even dropping in. You realize, of course, that he's probably the one who rescued your father. I'm wondering if he knows where your father is now. Getting a straight answer out of him seems to be a problem."

"I'm afraid you're right," Brand agreed.

"After that we'll — "

"Wait a minute," interrupted Brand. "We need to clarify just who's in charge here."

"You are, of course," she replied. "After that we'll — "

"Hold on," said Brand. "If I'm the one in charge

then I make the decisions."

"Fine," said Ember. "Make a decision."

"Very well. We'll do exactly as you've said."

With that they both hooted until Brand sank to the floor, groaning in pain and clutching his stitched-up belly. Shadrel, who had been hanging about the balcony, got caught up in the spirit of the moment and went howling gleefully through the corridors, causing such a disturbance that King Briais himself had to be summoned to settle the young prince down.

The day set for their departure finally arrived. Ember, dreading a large and noisy crowd of humans, suggested that they avoid the situation altogether.

"Let's sneak out before they wake," she said to Brand in the early hours of the morning.

But at daybreak, when they peered over the balcony's edge, they were greeted by a sea of people camped around the castle as far as the eye could see.

"So much for your low-profile exit," said Brand.

The humans of Kowtow had turned the event into a countrywide celebration. It wasn't until Ember and Brand had endured two full-course meals, a series of what King Briais called sporting events (which amounted to people chasing, kicking, or throwing round, colorful objects), and a long, rather tedious ceremony in which Yemah had been chosen to give the farewell speech, that they were permitted to leave. With Fiske beside them translating into Common Tongue, Yemah's address went something like this:

"I speak for all people when I say how honored we have been to have these fine dragons among us. I am sure you will join with me in wishing them a speedy, successful journey with fair weather and the wind at their backs.

"It has been my personal pleasure," he continued, "to travel with these courageous and noble dragons for many days. During our journey — "

At this point Yemah gave a rather long-winded version of their adventures from his human point of view. The tale was over-dramatized and filled with bright but irrelevant descriptions.

At last he concluded with "Goodbye, dear friends. May your homeward journey be pleasant and free from danger."

With that the entire assembly burst into wild cheers, hoots, and whistles that seemed to go on forever. When the gaiety subsided to a tolerable level, King Briais stepped forward, looking up at the balcony where Prince Shadrel smiled from under Brand's wing. He waited patiently for the hand-waving and head-bobbing of the crowd to end. Then he began to speak.

"Brand, son of my dear friend, Skortch, your friendship with my son has affected you in more ways than you realize. The ancient magic of the Dragon Lords has kindled a change within you. It is a gift that you have earned. In time you will discover what that gift is. Use it wisely, and only for good. Remember that those whose love and respect you rejoice with you. Farewell, till we meet again."

Ember had no idea what the gift was, but trusting King Briais as she now did, she was sure it would be something wonderful. Around them, the humans went wild with joy. As she stood gazing out at more peculiar little creatures than had ever appeared in her nightmares, she knew that she no longer felt any kind of anger, or even dislike.

It wasn't until the sun sank low in the western sky that she and Brand finally bid goodbye to Kowtow, the land without dragons.

They spent the next four days traveling back across the Great Sea. When they grew tired, Brand called forth a migrating grey whale. She was slow, but she carried them willingly, singing as she moved through the waves. Then came the desert. This time they crossed it more easily — due, Ember figured, to the fact that they were stronger than before, free of burdens, and more experienced in travel. They arrived upon Cidrok's mountain one clear evening just as darkness fell.

The old dragon was expecting them.

He insisted they stay overnight so that he could give them advice on how to protect themselves in any future encounter. (Or did he mean, Ember wondered, advice on how to stay out of trouble?) At dawn he began. He talked of history, politics, and the art of combat. He told them when to fight and when to fly, and explained that there is no shame in retreating if you live to win another day. (If you don't, Ember wondered, does that make you a coward?) He told them that magic is a tool that can be used for good or evil, and that not all men are evil, just as not all dragons are good.

Then he revealed that the only way they would ever have lasting peace in the land was if they brought back the rule of the Dragon Lords.

"But that doesn't make any sense," protested Ember. "It was a Dragon Lord who caused all this trouble in the first place."

"You're right, young one," Cidrok admitted. "But that was our mistake. No one creature — man or dragon — can handle that much power. From now on there will be a council — made up of men and dragons — that will have the authority to dethrone an evil Dragon Lord. We won't make that same mistake again."

"We?" asked Ember. "You make it sound like you were there."

A small puff of smoke escaped the old dragon's nostrils and he shifted his heavy body. But he did not respond. Instead, he changed the subject to Brand's father, Skortch.

"I believe he has gone to FarNorth," the old dragon explained, "where war is unknown, and much emphasis is placed on learning — and on healing, both of body and spirit."

"Licea. . ." Ember said softly, half to herself, "who has healed only one other dragon."

"What is that?" asked the old dragon.

"Pardon me," she replied. "I was just talking to myself."

It was time for them to go. They rose and moved slowly to the entrance of the cave. "Have you left anything out, Cidrok?" Ember asked, as they stood on the mountaintop, ready to depart. "Is there something you haven't told us?"

Cidrok guffawed gleefully. "I certainly hope so," he said.

They rose on beating wings until he was only a small black speck upon a silver peak.

"Farewell, hope of dragonkind," whispered

something in the wind.

"Did you say something, Brand?" Ember wondered aloud, but received no reply except the cawing of the jackdaw at her tail.

By evening the Blackrock Mountains were just a backdrop and they were coasting over Grass Land, within roaring distance of home.

The sun was sinking low. Shades of pink and gold adorned the western sky. Shadows stretched and grew. The air cooled, and flameflies dipped and darted. Ember followed Brand to where the stream had slowed and pooled. They landed on the bank and drank till they were filled.

"Take a look at yourself," Ember said, nodding at the pond's clear surface.

She wondered if Brand would roar aloud or chuckle with quiet delight. For he would see reflected there a transformation she had witnessed these past few days, like the unfurling of a scarlet moonrose in the night.

Brand's shoulders had widened. His chest had deepened. His legs, wings, neck and tail had thickened and lengthened. Vivid red scales now flamed like suns. His snout, feet, and wingtips had blackened to stand out in stark contrast, like night to day. In short, Brand was no longer a Scout dragon. The Dragon Lords' ancient magic had transformed him into a Father, able to have children of his own.

Brand stared, mesmerized, into the pool for so long that Ember grew alarmed.

Then a single tear slipped from his eye and trickled down his snout to drip upon the water's silken lid. The ripples sparkled as they spread.

"It's a gift," Brand whispered. "Such an incredible gift. I had no idea."

Ember felt tears well beneath her eyelids and struggled to gain control of her feelings.

"We've been around humans so long we're starting to act just like them," she grumbled.

"Is that so bad?" wondered Brand.

They gazed in awe and amazement at the two magnificent and fully adult dragons reflected in the pool. Finally Brand lifted his head, straightened his splendid back, and spoke.

"Some day I will meet Herd Father again. And when I do, I'm going to confront him — one full-grown to another. I'll tell him what a fine brave dragon he truly is, and how I've always admired him. Then I will ask him to withdraw his edict of death."

"Why don't you tell him he's a bully who terrorizes his mates and abuses his children, and if he doesn't relent, you'll knock him into the next cycle?"

"I suppose that's a more honest approach, all right."

They stood for a moment in quiet contemplation.

"Are you hungry?" Brand asked.

"A little."

"I'll be back with something soon," he said.

"I'll wait for you here."

Ember stepped back, felt the rush of air from his lift and heard the thunder of his wings. She bent to the water for one last refreshing sip. Then she turned, raising her face toward the glory of the dying day. Before, there had been just the clear evening air and a great span of emptiness as far as the wide horizon. Now, bright as a star aflame, one red dragon soared alone against the sun-streaked sky.

Vicki Blum lives in Calgary, Alberta, where she can look at the mountains and imagine dragons soaring over them. She enjoys walking, exercising and spending time with her two grandchildren. As an elementary-school librarian, she loves working with books and doing workshops with young writers. Her fantasy adventures — *The Mermaid Secret* and the five books in her best-selling Unicorn Collection — continue to enchant young readers.

Also by Vicki Blum

Wish Upon a Unicorn

Arica falls through a crack in her grandmother's floor — and into Bundelag, a world of fairies, trolls, elves and unicorns, where the unicorns need her help.

ISBN 0-590-51519-5

Book One in the Unicorn Collection

The Shadow Unicorn

Arica returns to the magical land of Bundelag to find that evil Raden — helped by the Shadow unicorn — has turned the other unicorns to stone. All but one . . .

ISBN 0-439-98706-7

Book Two in the Unicorn Collection

The Land Without Unicorns

The precious *Book of Fairies* must be retrieved from the dangerous lands of South Bundelag. Can Arica trust the Shadow unicorn to help her?

ISBN 0-439-98863-2

Book Three in the Unicorn Collection

The Promise of the Unicorn

Raden has poisoned Arica's mother. Arica must brave Dragon Island to find the rainbow flower that can save her.

ISBN 0-439-98967-1

Book Four in the Unicorn Collection

A Gathering of Unicorns

Even with Arica's help, can the magical creatures of North Bundelag defend themselves against invaders from the South?

ISBN 0-439-97417-8

Book Five in the Unicorn Collection

The Mermaid Secret

Twins Kallie and Danya must help a mermaid to return the Jewel of Life to Ayralon, a magical undersea world.

ISBN 0-439-96916-6

"This story is wonderfully captivating — mermaids, twins, adventures, dolphins, magic and villains. It is a perfect fantasy."

— *Canadian Materials*